This is going to turn out badly, she thought, panicking. *It always turns out badly, and I'm going to wish I hadn't come.*

But she couldn't turn back now. H__d already seen her. She forced h_____ ___ empty hands flutter___

This par_____ __ after a long absenc___ _____ ____ ___, or at least shake h_____ ___ldn't let her. The distance b_____ them just seemed too vast.

Not that he was rushing toward her with open arms. Jack Bristow stood where he was, letting her come to him.

She covered the final few feet, stopping awkwardly at arm's length. He hadn't mentioned her lateness, so maybe this was a good start after all. She searched his face for a sign.

"Hi, Dad," she ventured at last. "Sorry I'm late. I got here as soon as I could."

Jack twitched his head slightly. Annoyance? Dismissal? Forgiveness? She didn't have a clue.

"Hello, Sydney," he said coolly.

ALIAS™

FATHER FIGURE

LAURA PEYTON ROBERTS

AN ORIGINAL PREQUEL NOVEL BASED ON THE

HIT TV SERIES CREATED BY J. J. ABRAMS

BANTAM BOOKS
NEW YORK ✳ TORONTO ✳ LONDON ✳ SYDNEY ✳ AUCKLAND

Alias: Father Figure

A Bantam Book / November 2003

Text and cover art copyright © 2003 by Touchstone Television

ISBN: 0-553-49404-X

Visit us on the Web! www.randomhouse.com

Published simultaneously in the United States and Canada

Bantam Books is an imprint of Random House Children's Books, a
division of Random House, Inc. BANTAM BOOKS and the rooster
colophon are registered trademarks of Random House, Inc. Bantam
Books, New York, New York.

PRINTED IN THE UNITED STATES OF AMERICA

OPM 10 9 8 7 6 5 4 3 2 1

ALIAS™

FATHER FIGURE

I've seen a lot of things in this business, very few of them good.

It didn't start out that way. I was like any idealistic recruit once—maybe more idealistic than most.

But that was a long time ago. Now all I want is **out**.

Out of the CIA, out of SD-6, out of this point-less chaos some fool dubbed "intelligence."

So if the report I've just heard is true, if Reginald Wilson has actually recruited my only child into SD-6, heads are going to roll. When I get back to L.A., somebody had better have a **very good** explanation, because if anything's happened to Sydney . . .

I will **not** have my daughter mixed up in this. Not after everything I've done to keep her **out** of it. I want to see Sydney **safe**. Normal. **Happy**.

One of us ought to be.

1

"**YOU DO NOT WANT** to mess with me," Sydney Bristow said, struggling to keep her voice light. "Really. You have no idea."

"Or what?" Burke Wells teased, dangling a heavy book just out of her reach. "You'll beat me up?"

"There are so many possibilities. Let's just keep it vague."

One strawberry blond brow hiked suggestively, emphasizing the mischievous gleam in Burke's hazel eyes. "If you're going to put it like that, I'd rather hear you spell it out."

Sydney lunged across the library table, catching her hip bone on its sharp edge as she tried to snag the book. Her grab came up short.

Burke's playful smile grew broader. He waggled the book tantalizingly.

"What is this? Junior high?" she burst out, exasperated. "I have to study, Burke, and this is the only day I can do it. You said you had to study too."

He relented at last, handing over her history textbook. "You're so serious today."

"You ought to try it sometime," she said, still peeved.

She never would have agreed to go to the library with him in the first place if he hadn't assured her they'd study for Friday's American history quiz. Friday probably seemed a long way off to him, but Sydney's perception of time had changed radically since she'd become an agent-in-training with the top-secret branch of the CIA known as SD-6. Her handler, Reginald Wilson, was forever calling her in for briefings or sending her off on missions, making it imperative for her to take full advantage of any spare second she could call her own. Her most recent mission in Oahu had left her so far behind in her classes she was starting to worry she'd never catch up.

"It's just a quiz," Burke said. "You act like it's the final."

"It *will* be the final, in seventeen days, and I don't know any of this stuff!"

"Can you believe it's almost summer?" he asked, changing the subject. "What have you got planned?"

"Besides repeating this class?"

Burke shook his head, his red hair brushing his broad shoulders. "Try to lighten up for just five minutes, okay? Look around you. We're practically the only ones here."

Sydney sighed, casting a glance around the huge group study room. The fact that Burke was right changed nothing. If she'd learned anything during her freshman year of college, it was that the number of people in the library was always inversely proportional to the beauty of the weather outside—and the sunshine that Sunday morning was gorgeous. The students with any control over their schedules would wait until dark to even think about studying. Unfortunately, Sydney wasn't a member of their privileged ranks.

She sighed again. "At least we aren't bothering anyone."

"You need to learn to relax," he said. "What are you so wound up about?"

"I have to learn this material!" She tapped the textbook in front of her. "If you already know it all, why don't you test me?"

"You mean ask you questions? Like a pretend quiz?"

"Go ahead. Give me your best shot."

Not that it's going to take a SWAT team to pick me off in this class, she thought, watching Burke pull the book across the table and start flipping its pages. *American history ought to be my best subject. After all, I am a spy for the U.S. government.*

She'd do better if Professor Baldridge stuck to concepts and major events, or even rough chronologies, but his midterm had demonstrated an obsessive fascination with dates, exact locations, and equally forgettable trivia.

"Okay," Burke said slowly, moving his finger down a page. "Where was President Kennedy shot?"

"Texas."

"Texas is a big state."

"Dallas," she said, gaining confidence. "*Downtown* Dallas."

"Date?" Burke asked.

"November 22, 1963."

"Name of his assassin?"

"Lee Harvey Oswald."

Burke snorted. "Right. If you believe in fairy tales."

Sydney stifled a groan. For a second there, they were almost accomplishing something.

"Did you see that show on public TV the other night?" he went on. "The one where those photographers proved that a bullet from the School Book Depository would have created a shadow trail visible in film shot from the grassy knoll?"

"Are you sure it wasn't the Sci Fi Channel?"

"Very funny," he said, undeterred. "You should have seen it. They found this new way of digitally enhancing the photographs taken that day, and then they did tests with dummy shots under the same atmospheric conditions and . . ."

Another conspiracy theory, she thought, tuning out. *And this one's not even original.* At least when Burke got worked up about CNN as a form of mind control, or the fast food industry's plot to supersize Americans, or even the subversive nature of soap, she found his theories amusing. *He must be running out of material.*

"I mean, the whole idea that some wacko with a gun, working completely alone, could bring down a president . . ."

Right. Because that's never happened before.

She wondered if Burke had any idea how young and naïve his relentless suspicions of the government, the media, corporate America, and just about everything else made him sound.

Noah has his flaws, but at least he's serious,

she thought, gazing off into space. *The big question is, is he serious about me?*

Ever since they'd returned from Hawaii, Agent Hicks had been running hot and cold, affectionate one day, distant the next. She understood they needed to keep their relationship secret from SD-6, but sometimes it felt like Noah was trying to hide it from himself too.

"Sydney?" Burke said, breaking into her thoughts. "Syd, are you still with me?"

"Huh? Oh, sorry. I might have checked out during the satellite coordinates of the overpass nearest the motorcade."

"But that overpass is key! If somebody had—" He stopped in midsentence, reading her expression. "No, *I'm* sorry. You keep telling me you need to study, and I keep fooling around. I must be driving you crazy."

"Not exactly *crazy*," she said, not wanting to hurt his feelings.

"It's just that I never get to see you." An impish smile curled his lips. "At least not as much of you as I'd like."

Sydney smiled back at his innuendo. "I'm not saying you'll ever succeed with that, but making me fail this quiz won't help."

"Which is why we need to study!" he said,

thumping the pages of her open book. "What have I been telling you since we got here?"

For the next hour, Burke was a reformed character, peppering her with sample quiz questions. She did pretty well at first, but once he got past the easy stuff she started falling apart. She remembered the dates and motivations behind the Korean War but forgot the difficult names of the cities involved. She defined *Cold War* perfectly but couldn't come up with the journalist who'd coined the phrase. When she drew a blank on the Democrat President Reagan defeated to win his second term, she lost patience with herself.

"I was alive then!" she cried, disgusted. "If I can't even remember what happened during my lifetime, what chance do I have with the rest of that stuff?"

"You're too hard on yourself," Burke said. "Most of what you missed is so trivial that no one but Baldridge would ask it. Besides, you don't usually have problems remembering things."

"No," she admitted reluctantly. In fact, she was kind of a legend at SD-6 for all the languages, skills, and classified data she'd already learned.

"You're working too many hours—that's the problem," he said with genuine concern. "You need to take more time off. Give your brain a rest."

"Work! Oh no!" she exclaimed, jumping up with her eyes on her watch. "I've got to be there in half an hour."

"Be where? Not the *bank*?"

"Overtime filing." The lies she used to hide her activities with SD-6 became more automatic every day. "It's good money."

"Maybe so, but can't they do it without you? You need the break more than the cash."

"I *do* need the cash!"

"All right, don't take my head off. I just hate seeing you stressed."

He looked so sincerely worried that Sydney was ashamed of herself.

"Will I see you later?" he asked. "Maybe for dinner tonight?"

"Sorry. I wish I could, but I have . . . stuff," she finished lamely, jamming books into her backpack. "I'll have to see you tomorrow in class."

She escaped before he could argue, rushing from the library into the warm sunshine outside. It wasn't that she didn't *want* to spend time with Burke, she told herself as she hurried across campus toward her dorm. It was just that she had no idea how long Wilson was going to keep her that day.

Plus, Noah might call later. . . .

The thought made her stop in her tracks, nearly causing a collision with a bicyclist following too closely behind. She wasn't putting off Burke to leave herself open for Noah?

No, she decided, relieved. They were two completely different people, but she honestly cared for them both. That was why she still couldn't choose between them—or tell them about each other. Saying good-bye to either one would be an impossible task.

But I still have to do it, she thought. *And soon.*

Sydney heaved a sigh and increased her pace to a trot.

I really wish I knew how.

* * *

"Get a lot done at the library?" Francie Calfo asked as Sydney burst into their dorm room and dropped her backpack on the floor.

"Yep," Sydney said, beginning to pull off her tank top. "And now I have exactly five minutes to get dressed for the bank."

She heard Francie's exasperated sigh through the shirt still bunched around her ears. *Here it comes,* she thought, tensing.

Francie wasn't just Sydney's roommate, she

was her best friend. But there was one thing about Sydney that Francie didn't like: her job. Like everyone else outside SD-6, Francie believed Sydney was a lowly clerk at Credit Dauphine, and she hated the way the bank treated Sydney—calling her in at all hours and sending her off to catch up the filing at out-of-town branches.

"I can't believe your boss is making you work another Sunday," Francie said. "It's a *bank,* for crying out loud! Hasn't he heard of bankers' hours?"

Sydney braced herself and pulled the shirt off her head. As anticipated, her friend's eyes were full of annoyance.

"I have to go, Francie."

"Fine, go. I wouldn't dream of stopping you." Turning her back to use the mirror inside her closet door, Francie began brushing her black hair, twisting it into a stylish knot.

Okay, I didn't see that coming, Sydney thought, pausing with one leg out of her shorts. *Isn't this the part where she tries to talk me out of working?*

It was almost a weekend ritual: Sydney rushing off to work, Francie complaining about all the plans Sydney was ruining, Sydney making foolish promises about coming home early, Francie sulking as Sydney ran out the door . . .

"Maybe I can get off early," Sydney ventured.

"Don't bother on my account. I have other plans."

Francie anchored her twist with a chopstick, then picked up a red lip liner and began tracing her full mouth. Sydney watched, temporarily sidetracked. Was Francie going someplace without her? And if so, why wasn't she giving up details?

"So, you, uh . . . you look awfully nice for Sunday afternoon in the dorms," she said at last. "Is that top new?"

Francie turned back to face her. "I got it yesterday. You like?"

Hitting a model's pose, she spun around in the limited floor space between the foot of her twin bed and her open closet door, showing off her new red camisole. She had combined it with low-rise jeans and red canvas slides, her look cute, summery, and carefree. Sydney tried not to envy her roommate as she opened her own closet door and removed the boring khakis she invariably wore to the "bank."

"I do like it," she replied. "Where'd you get it?"

"There's the cutest store on Sunset!" Francie said, returning to her lipstick. "I wanted to go to the mall, but Shauna said we had to try Hollywood and she was totally right."

"Shauna?" Sydney reached for her standard blue button-down, then, in a fit of summer rebellion, grabbed a pink peasant blouse instead.

"That girl I told you about from my biology lecture."

"I don't remember." Sydney was pretty sure there was nothing *to* remember, but she didn't want to rile Francie up again.

"She and Carly and I all sit in back, where the droning's a little less painful."

"So you and Shauna went shopping yesterday?"

"And Carly. While you were at the bank. As usual." Francie cast a brief, accusing look back over her shoulder. "Don't you ever miss having a life?"

"All the time. But you know I have to work."

"Right. Of course!" Francie said sarcastically. "Because if Credit Dauphine ever had a paper out of order or—God help us—in the wrong drawer, the very fabric of society would rip asunder, chaos would fill the gap, and life as we know it would be totally, completely over."

Sydney pressed her lips together. "Been practicing that speech long?"

"About a week," Francie admitted, shutting her closet door and turning around with a pleased smile on her face. "Good, wasn't it?"

"If the drama department only knew." Picking

up a hairbrush, Sydney began slicking her straight brown hair into her usual work ponytail.

Francie eased past her to get to the door. "See you later," she said, reaching for the knob.

"Wait! You didn't even tell me where you're going."

"Didn't I? I'm meeting Shauna and Carly for lunch, then I think we're seeing a matinee. Or we might just kill time watching guys until the dance clubs open."

"But it's Sunday!" Sydney protested.

Francie shook her head. "Tell it to your boss," she suggested, slipping out the door.

* * *

I am not *jealous,* Sydney told herself as she rode the elevator from the underground parking garage into the heart of SD-6. *That would be ridiculous.*

She and Francie weren't joined at the hip. In fact, it would be weird if they didn't do things with other people sometimes.

Except that I never do. At least not with anyone I can tell Francie about.

The elevator stopped, its doors opening onto a small white room with a black circle painted on its floor. Sydney strode to the circle's center and stared straight ahead, letting retinal scanning verify her identity. The computer cleared her and a pair of doors opened on the opposite side of the room, admitting her onto the main floor of SD-6 headquarters.

Her pulse quickened with excitement as she walked through the cavernous space on her way to Wilson's glass-walled office. SD-6 agents worked at numerous small desks in this relatively open part of the building, and tucked in among the raw concrete columns, computer monitors glowed despite the fact it was Sunday. Their light made the windowless space seem warmer, and suddenly Sydney didn't feel as bad about missing the afternoon with Francie. Criminals didn't take Sundays off, and neither did the CIA—at least not the ultracovert branch she belonged to. Her heels clicked purposefully as she passed the large conference room, skirted a smaller research area, and headed down the final hallway, where Wilson's door stood open.

Sydney's CIA handler was sitting behind his mahogany desk, the casual tilt of his chair belying the edgy energy crackling just beneath his surface. Wilson was always awake, always on, always working some new angle to bring down the bad guys—which explained why the silver strands were winning their war with his chestnut hair. He motioned her into his office, and Sydney suddenly realized there was someone else in the room. In one of two chairs facing Wilson, Noah Hicks turned to meet her gaze, a hint of smugness around his lips betraying his enjoyment of her obvious surprise.

"Right on time!" Wilson greeted her. "You remember Agent Hicks from your Paris mission."

"Of course," Sydney said, not about to mention where else she remembered him from. "I didn't realize you'd be here today, Agent Hicks," she added, taking the seat beside his.

Her heart had begun racing the way it always did when Noah was around, making her wonder if she was crazy to still be seeing Burke. Burke was sweet, and honest, and open; objectively, he was probably more handsome, with that hippie-throwback-meets-male-model thing he had going. But compared to the comfortable feeling Burke gave her, being next to Noah felt like a fireworks finale. Ever since she'd first spotted him, working out in one of SD-6's training rooms, he'd taken her breath away. He was older than she was, for one thing, and he carried that experience in his face—in the wariness of his brown eyes and the scar underlining one side of his jaw. His wavy brown hair was cropped short, all business, yet when he got excited he raked it with both hands until it stuck out everywhere. But the most magnetic thing about Noah was his obvious self-confidence. It was palpable. It was infuriating.

It was irresistible.

Sydney waited expectantly now to see his familiar sly grin, or even a slight wink—any little sign that he was glad to see her too—but Noah's attention had already fastened back on Wilson as if she wasn't even in the room.

Score one for Burke, she thought, annoyed. She hadn't expected a make-out session in Wilson's office, but would it have killed him to say hello?

"I have a new assignment for you, Sydney," Wilson said. "I've already briefed Agent Hicks, and he can fill you in on the details."

"All right," she said, striving to keep her voice level. "Am I reporting to him on this, then?"

"No, still to me. But since you'll be on assignment together, you'll obviously collaborate closely with Agent Hicks. He may have instructions for you in the field."

"Fine," she said, relieved. She was happy for the chance to spend more time with Noah, but being in charge of a mission didn't exactly bring out his warm, fuzzy side. "What are we working on?"

"Congratulations," Wilson said ironically, passing her a large envelope across his desk. "You've been accepted as a student intern at SpaceSoft Technologies. Or rather, your alias, Kristin Jarvis, has. Your starting papers are in there, fake IDs, a map, parking permit, et cetera. Don't drive your own car, obviously."

"Don't drive it where, exactly?"

"SST is a big software firm here in Los Angeles. They're private sector, but they do a lot of work for the government. High-tech military applications. Classified contracts."

Sydney thought she saw where he was headed. "And you think they're leaking intel?"

"Nothing that straightforward." Wilson pushed back in his chair. "I'm not sure *what* they're doing. But there's a rumor floating around that they're freelancing in missile guidance systems."

"Freelancing how?"

"That's what we're going to find out," Noah said, finally speaking to her.

Wilson nodded. "Once you're in the building, you should have plenty of chances to look around. Keep an eye on the CEO, Owen Vincent. Everyone agrees he's the brains on the technical end, but we know surprisingly little about him. His photo is in your file. Memorize it."

"Will do," Sydney said.

Wilson continued to hold her gaze, as if to make certain she understood the gravity of her mission before delivering his final instruction:

"I want to know *exactly* what SpaceSoft is working on—and who they're planning to sell it to."

2

SYDNEY AND NOAH RODE the SD-6 elevator in silence, staring straight ahead. She suspected he was keeping quiet because conversations in the elevator might be monitored, but if he wasn't talking to her, then she sure wasn't speaking to him. When the doors finally opened on the parking garage, Sydney exited without a word and headed straight for her white Mustang.

"Hey, Syd. Wait!"

She heard him run up behind her as she pulled her keys from her purse.

"Oh, *now* you want to talk to me," she said, turning to face him.

The impassive look he'd worn in Wilson's office had completely vanished, replaced by a boyish grin. "Of course I do. It's just that I couldn't before."

"You mean you wouldn't," she grumbled. "You could at least have said hello."

"I did."

"No, you didn't."

"I think I did."

"Then you're wrong."

Noah's expression hardened momentarily, the way it always did when they argued. Then, to her relief, he took a couple of steps forward, moving very close.

"Hey, Sydney?" he said softly.

"What?"

"Hello."

There was a hint of puppy dog in his usually guarded eyes. His voice held the same longing she felt for him.

"Hello," she said, crumbling.

"You want to have dinner with me?"

"Now?"

He glanced at his watch. "I guess it's a little early, but by the time we get to a restaurant—"

"No. What I meant was, is that okay? For the two of us to be seen together?"

"No one's going to see us. And if they do, who cares?"

"I'm thinking Wilson might."

Noah dismissed her concern with a flick of one wrist. "Did he or did he not tell me to fill you in on the details of the SST assignment?"

"He did," Sydney admitted cautiously.

"And are you or are you not able to eat and listen at the same time?"

Sydney's cheeks dimpled despite her attempts to maintain a straight face. "I can usually manage that."

"So there you have it!" Noah concluded, smiling back, "Wilson practically *ordered* us to eat out." He lowered his voice to a stagy whisper. "It's a matter of national security!"

* * *

"Still worried someone will see us?" Noah teased two hours later.

The hostess had buried them at the back of the dark Chinese restaurant, so far out of sight that even their waiter had forgotten about them. They'd been sipping tea for the past half hour, picking at fortune cookie crumbs and leftover crispy noodles.

"I guess we're probably safe," Sydney admitted.

Noah leaned forward conspiratorially. "I hear these booths are bulletproof. All the cool spies eat here."

Sydney rolled her eyes, but the fact that he was actually joking about espionage eased the last bit of tension from her body. There was no way Noah would be fooling around if there was even a remote chance they were under surveillance.

"I guess you'd better fill me in on whatever's left to know about SST," she said. "I have to be leaving soon."

Noah looked surprised. "What's left to know?"

"You tell me. You're the one who wanted to fill me in on all those details over dinner."

He laughed, the sound unexpectedly loud in their tiny corner. "I just wanted to hang out with you."

"I know. But there have to be more details. Wilson hardly told me anything."

Noah shrugged. "That's because he doesn't know much. Could be there's nothing to know. You and I are going to find out."

"Well, if I'm supposed to be a student intern," Sydney persisted, "how are you getting in?"

"They got me a full-time job, punching the

clock. Strictly drudge work, but one of us has to be there all day and you're only on afternoons. Your schedule's in the envelope Wilson gave you."

"Only afternoons?" she said, surprised. "This assignment gets better all the time."

"How so?"

"Right now I'm about a semester behind on a quarter's worth of work. If Wilson sent me away again before finals, or even put me at SpaceSoft full time . . ." She shook her head. "This way I might actually get to attend classes."

Noah chuckled. "I hate to break this to you, Syd, but ditching is part of the college experience. Most students actually enjoy it."

"Maybe I would too, if I got to choose *when* I ditched," she retorted. "Maybe if my schedule wasn't so completely, totally out of my hands that—"

"I get the picture," he interrupted. "Listen, there is one more thing. Wilson told you not to drive your own car, but he forgot to mention you should work in disguise."

"In disguise? Disguised as what?"

"Disguised as your alias, Kristin Jarvis, whatever she looks like. Wear a wig. Use some extra makeup. You don't want to attract attention; you just don't want to look like yourself. Not for a gig in L.A."

Sydney nodded, seeing his point. It could be awkward if one of her SST coworkers recognized her somewhere else—entering Credit Dauphine, for example.

"I keep my disguise kit in a locker at the school gym," she told him. "I'll come up with something."

"Good. Rent a car and leave it parked nearby. Be sure to rent it as Kristin."

"I'm a trainee; I'm not stupid."

He sighed. "I didn't say you can't take care of yourself. It's just . . ."

"I know. I worry about you too."

"Me?" he scoffed. "I've been at this forever compared to you."

"That's the problem. The longer you're in, the more enemies you make."

Noah grimaced. "Way to pump up a guy's confidence."

"You know I'm right."

"Maybe," he said at last. "But I think I'll survive this mission." A sudden twinkle lit his eyes. "If you're worried about me, though, I could use an armed escort to my apartment. Just to make sure I get inside safely."

"I'm not armed."

"I'll lend you my gun."

He looked so comically hopeful that Sydney had to laugh.

"Not tonight," she said regretfully. "As much as I'd love to finally see your apartment, I have to get back to my dorm. I've got a mountain of homework, and my roommate will worry if I get home late."

"You're already late," Noah pointed out.

"If I get home later, then."

"You'll have to be a *little* later."

"Why?"

"Because I haven't even kissed you yet."

Their eyes locked across the table and the restaurant melted away. Sydney's pulse twitched in her throat. Her heartbeat thumped in her ears.

I love him, she thought. *I must. How else could he make me so crazy?*

"Well," she murmured. "A few minutes never killed anybody."

Noah smiled and reached for her hand. "Don't let Wilson hear you say that."

* * *

That's weird, Sydney thought, opening her door to find an empty dorm room. *I can't believe Francie's not back by now.*

She glanced around, confirming everything was as they'd left it. And then she remembered.

She did say something about going dancing.

Not that Sydney had fully believed her. Francie loved to dance, but Sunday night hanging out at the dorms was a ritual for the whole building. That was when everyone put on their comfiest sweats, brewed their strongest coffee, and settled in for the long night of cramming required to catch up for Monday. Granted, there tended to be at least as much running to the microwave for popcorn and s'mores as actual studying, but that was what made it fun.

If she was serious about dancing, she could have at least invited me to meet them, Sydney thought, feeling jealous again. She hadn't known about Shauna and Carly for twelve hours yet, and they were already stealing her best friend.

Sydney sighed as she opened a drawer and started digging for her most broken-in sweatpants.

Would it have killed Wilson to mention that spies don't have social lives?

If anything, her recruiter had implied that joining SD-6 would give her a whole new circle of friends to rely on, but the only one making new friends was Francie. Sydney still wasn't even convinced Wilson wouldn't be mad when he found out about her dinner with Noah.

If *he finds out,* she amended. *I'm not going to tell him.*

She located the sweatpants and turned to toss them onto her bed, and that was when she noticed the blinking light on her answering machine.

"Francie!" she exclaimed happily, rushing over and pressing the button. If Francie and her new friends were dancing at a club somewhere, Sydney still had time to take a quick shower and join them. Maybe she'd actually *like* Shauna and Carly. Maybe they could all hang out together. . . .

"Sydney, this is your father." The cold, precise voice on her answering machine drained the air out of her lungs. "I have some time off work and I'll be in town to spend it with you. Let's have dinner at the Union Hotel tomorrow. Six o'clock. I'll meet you in the lobby."

"No way!" she groaned, dropping backward onto her bed. She had barely even heard from her father since she'd started college—and she wasn't sure she wanted that to change.

We'll only start fighting again. We always do.

When she was a little girl, after her mother died, Sydney had tried everything she could think of to gain her father's attention and turn him into the close, loving parent she missed so desperately. She had long since given up hope.

All Jack Bristow cared about was his employer, Jennings Aerospace, and the stupid airplane parts he sold on trips all over the world. Last she'd heard, Jennings had packed him off on a sales tour of South America; no one had even bothered to tell her when he'd be back. Not that she'd been surprised. Making business calls had always been more important to him than calling his own daughter. His home base was still L.A., but he didn't even keep an apartment anymore, choosing instead to live in hotels on the rare occasions he was actually in town.

I can't believe he's showing up now! Two weeks before finals. And does he even ask about my schedule? What does he think? That I'll just drop everything?

In fairness, his ignorance of SD-6 made it impossible for him to know exactly how much he was asking her to drop, but Sydney didn't feel like cutting him any slack. An angry flush rose to her cheeks at his lack of consideration.

This is so typical. It's always about what's convenient for him. "I have another business trip, Sydney. Don't worry—you'll like boarding school."

How can he believe I'd even want to see him?

That was the part that made her maddest—his arrogant assumption that she'd fall all over herself with joy. Did he really think she was still young enough to believe things could change between them? If history was any guide, he'd show up for a couple of days, take her to some nice restaurants, then neglect her for the rest of the year.

I'd be crazy to want to see him!

Sydney buried her face in her hands, drawing long, jagged breaths against the growing pressure in her chest. There was only one thing worse than her father's assumption that she'd want him around: the fact that he was right.

She couldn't help it. Maybe this time *would* be different. Maybe he'd finally changed.

Maybe you need to get your head examined, she thought, wiping at angry tears. But she already knew that, despite everything, she would welcome him again, would act happy to see him, and would drop as much as she could.

What choice do I have?

There had been such a hole in her life since her mother died.

A hole only a father could fill.

3

"HERE WE GO," SYDNEY murmured, driving her silver rental car into the huge parking lot of Space-Soft Technologies. Her heart raced with excitement to be on another mission, but the face in her rearview mirror didn't betray a thing.

Kristin Jarvis was a blonde, Sydney had decided, with overlined lips and a thing for mascara. Peering out from between such thick black lashes, Sydney's newly blue eyes seemed even more shocking. To become her alias she had opted for colored contact lenses and a tousled pixie-cut wig; add the extra makeup and she was practically a different person. Anyone used to her naturally brown eyes and long straight hair would walk past without looking twice.

Pulling into an empty parking space, Sydney checked her new look one last time, then let herself out and locked the car door. Heat radiated from the pavement, making the walk from the car to Space-Soft's lobby seem even farther than it was. The expansive landscaped parking lot sprawled at the base of SST's glass-clad building, an office tower over twenty stories high with a low pentagonal entry jutting out in front. Sydney headed directly for its front doors, the full skirt of her summery first-day dress swirling around her bare calves with every long, sure stride.

She felt a little less cocky when she noticed the security camera mounted on the front of the building and realized she was already under scrutiny. In almost the same moment, an automatic glass door opened, admitting her into the lobby.

Outside it was noisy, smoggy, and hot, but the lobby of SpaceSoft Technologies felt like an Asian retreat. The blue-green tint of the exterior glass filtered the glare from outside, softening it into a cool, soothing light that rippled across the black stone floor. Massive pots of graceful bamboo provided vertical accents and in the exact center of the floor, the stone gave way to a pentagonal sand garden, precisely raked in an intricately swirling pattern. Sydney was so taken by the contrast that several seconds passed before she noticed the dark-haired woman behind the ebony reception counter—or the armed security guard lounging against its end.

"Hi! I'm, uh . . . I'm Kristin Jarvis," Sydney said, momentarily thrown off her game by the unexpected beauty of her surroundings. She had expected a company full of engineers to run toward Formica and pocket protectors; the Zen thing was a big surprise. "I'm starting today? The intern?"

"Right." The woman held out her hand, palm up.

Sydney hesitated uncertainly, then flipped her own hand over to shake it. "Nice to meet you."

"Nice to meet you, too," came the amused reply. "But I need your paperwork."

"My paperwork! Of course!"

Digging into her purse, Sydney pulled out her letter of acceptance and handed it over.

"Driver's license?" the woman inquired. "Social security card?"

"Sure. Okay."

"My name is Rachel," the woman said, smiling. "Once you get signed in, I'll show you the ropes."

Sydney risked a closer look at her new supervisor. Rachel was younger than she'd appeared at first glance, late twenties at the most. Her severe black bangs and the black-framed glasses sliding down her small nose added years she didn't possess. Her clothes were both stylish and expensive, the junior executive look right out of a magazine.

"How do I get signed in?" Sydney asked, wishing she'd worn pumps instead of sandals.

Rachel motioned the security guard over to join them. "Frank'll show you. Frank, this is Kristin Jarvis. She needs her ID badge."

"Sure thing," Frank said, leering at Sydney.

"Down, boy." Rachel rolled her eyes. "Don't mind Frank," she told Sydney. "He's married. All show and no go."

"I have something I'd like to show *you*," Frank parried, turning his attention to Rachel.

"Uh-huh," said Rachel, unfazed. "It's good to have a dream. Now hurry up and help Kristin so I can get her started."

"I'd like to get *you* started."

"Wow," said Rachel. "Clever. You've caught me totally without a comeback. How about that ID?"

"Whatever." Frank took Sydney's identification cards from Rachel and motioned for Sydney to follow him out through a door at the back of the lobby. "I'll be back," he told Rachel as they left.

"Okay. Wouldn't want you to do anything crazy, like patrol the building."

"Patrol!" Frank scoffed to Sydney, leading the way down a carpeted hall. "If a perpetrator comes into the building, how's he going to enter?"

He gave Sydney a sharp glance, as if seriously expecting an answer. She shrugged helplessly.

"Through the *door,* that's how. Perps'll come in through the *lobby.*"

She managed a slight, uncertain smile, but inside she was laughing out loud. If all the guards were as brilliant as Frank, she and Noah should be pretty safe.

On the other hand, I *just came in through the lobby. Maybe Frank's not as dumb as he seems.*

"In here," he said brusquely, indicating a small, dingy room at the end of the hall. A beat-up metal desk and file cabinet gave the place a grungy ambiance. Using a key on a retractable chain, Frank opened the top file drawer and removed a blank fingerprint card, slapping it down on the desktop along with Sydney's fake IDs.

"You're, uh . . . you're taking my fingerprints?" she asked nervously as Frank added a pad of ink and some paper towels to the items on the desk. "What for?"

"For security," he said as if she were dense.

Apparently he saved his sexual harassment for Rachel. "What's the matter? Got a record?"

"Of course not!" she said quickly.

"Then what's the damage?"

"Nothing. I mean . . . go ahead."

The last thing she wanted was for SST to have her fingerprints, but causing a scene would raise suspicion. As Frank pushed her right index finger down on the ink, then moved it to the proper position on the card, Sydney fought back the urge to twist her hand, smudging the print into uselessness. For one thing, Frank had a death grip on her finger, rolling it back and forth with military precision. For another, there was no way she'd succeed with that ploy ten times.

"Relax," Frank said, his leer returning. "Tensing up only makes it worse."

Sydney submitted reluctantly, comforting herself by imagining all the ways she could make Frank scream. When he'd finished, he handed her a paper towel and told her to stand with her back to the wall and her toes on a piece of tape.

"Picture time!" he announced, pulling out a digital camera. "Smile pretty."

Sydney smiled, hoping her wig was still on straight. Disguises only worked because people rarely looked at each other closely. What if Frank suddenly noticed a strand of long brown hair escaping from beneath her short blond hairdo? What if he asked about contact lenses?

The sudden flash of the camera left her seeing purple spots.

"All right," he said. "I've got to go laminate this and make copies of your other IDs. Wait here until I get back."

Sydney nodded, relieved to see him go, especially since he'd left her fingerprint card lying out on the desk. Could she steal it, then convince him he'd taken it with him to the other room? No, he'd just make another one. Could she forge a new one somehow? What would she use for fingerprints?

The top drawer of the file cabinet was still unlocked. If there were any completed cards in there, perhaps she could put her name on someone else's. Sydney was moving toward the cabinet when Frank walked back into the room.

"Now you're official," he said, handing her a laminated ID card attached to a metal clip. KRISTIN JARVIS—INTERN and a photograph of a blonde she barely recognized were centered between the SST logo and a string of security code. "Make sure you wear that every day, and wear it where I can see it."

"All right," she said, clipping the ID to the front of her dress. "But you already know me, Frank."

"Wear it anyway. I'm not the only guard here, you know. Plus, I've got a lot of people to keep track of. Which reminds me, it's time for my patrol. Can you find your way back to Rachel?"

"No problem," Sydney said eagerly. If he left her in the room by herself . . .

But before she could finish the thought, Frank lifted her fingerprint card off the desk, put it in the drawer, and locked the file cabinet.

"You still here?" he said, turning around again.

"I was, uh . . . just leaving. Which way was it?"

She let Frank point her in the only possible direction, then set off to find Rachel.

"All done?" Rachel asked when Sydney reappeared in the lobby.

"Done with him, anyway," Sydney replied, letting her disgust creep into her voice.

"Don't I know it!" Rachel shook her head sadly. "Welcome to SST."

For the next hour, she explained Sydney's new duties to her. They spent fifty minutes on the proper way to answer the phone and transfer calls, and for the rest of the time Sydney learned how to use the electronic postage meter.

"Okay, so I answer the phones and put postage on outgoing mail," Sydney said. "What else?"

"Make copies," Rachel said. "Lots of copies.

These engineers always have some manual or other they want Xeroxed, but I can't show you the copy room now—somebody has to stay on the desk."

"You could just point me in that direction . . . ," Sydney suggested, sensing an opportunity to do some unsupervised exploring.

"There's really nothing to see. I'll show you later, when Jamia gets down here."

"Down from where?"

"Top floor," Rachel said. "Jamia is Mr. Vincent's secretary. He's out a lot, though, like today, which leaves her with time on her hands. The girls in word processing cover my breaks, but Jamia does it when he's not here, just for the change of scenery."

"Scenery? If Mr. Vincent's office is on the top floor, the view ought to be pretty nice."

"It is. I guess." Rachel looked a bit sheepish. "I've only been on that floor once. We aren't exactly encouraged to wander out of our work areas, so until I get promoted . . ."

Great, thought Sydney. *That ought to make my mission more challenging.*

"What else do I do?" she asked. "Besides the phone, the mail, and copies, I mean. Where's my computer?"

Rachel's sculpted brows drew together. "We do

have one *shared* computer. . . ." She gestured to a blank monitor. "But it's easier to use the typewriter for envelopes and labels. The secretaries type everything else."

"No, I mean, where will I be writing programs? I thought being an intern meant I'd work with the engineers."

Rachel gave her an incredulous look. "It means you have your foot in the door, and that's it. Do you have a degree in computer science?"

Sydney hesitated, not sure what lies Wilson had told in her internship application. "Not yet," she finally ventured.

"Well, I do," Rachel told her. "And I'm still answering the phone. Everyone here pays their dues."

"Gotcha," Sydney said, wondering how Wilson expected her to learn anything useful at the front desk. "Do you want me to take over the switchboard while you go on your break? We could save Jamia a trip."

"You think you're ready for it?" Rachel asked skeptically. "It's not as easy as it looks—especially when we get busy and all the lines light up at once."

"The phone hasn't been ringing that much," Sydney pointed out. "I'd think a big building like this would have a ton more calls coming in."

"Voice mail," Rachel said. "Best thing we ever

got. Most of our repeat callers use the automated system. But every now and then—"

The telephone rang, several lights on the switchboard blinking simultaneously.

"See what I mean?" Rachel asked, reaching for the handset.

"I have to use the ladies' room," Sydney whispered. "I'll just . . ." She pointed tentatively behind them, toward the hallway she'd walked through with Frank.

Rachel shook her head.

"SpaceSoft Technologies. This is Rachel," she said into the phone. "Will you please hold?" She punched another line. "SpaceSoft Technologies. Will you please hold? SpaceSoft Technologies . . ."

Sydney pointed toward the only other doorway at the back of the lobby. Rachel nodded, then gave her full attention to the phone. "Will you please hold?"

Sydney escaped down the second hallway, eager to do some looking around on her own. This new hallway was wider and much more opulent than the first, with burgundy carpeting and expensive prints on the walls. Only fifty feet from the lobby, it opened into a spacious atrium with two banks of elevators and a fountain in the center. Sydney moved slowly toward the ladies' room on the other side, taking in every detail.

A glass-fronted board on the wall nearest the fountain featured head shots of the principals of SST. Sydney veered course to get a better look at the photograph of Owen Vincent, which was almost identical to the one in the SpaceSoft brochure Wilson had provided. Vincent's features were slightly out of focus and entirely nondescript—just another serious-looking white guy in a gray suit and brown crew cut. Even his tie was boring.

Turning her attention to the elevators, Sydney noticed lighted displays above the doors, indicating that cars were in use on other floors, but so far none of them had come to the atrium, leaving her temporarily alone. A security camera mounted prominently in one corner made her worry she might be under surveillance, but she couldn't pass up such a golden opportunity. Changing directions abruptly, she walked to the elevators and pressed the call button.

Her timing was good; a car arrived almost instantly. But when the doors opened, Sydney found herself facing a group of middle-aged men in dress slacks and short-sleeved oxfords, SST badges hanging askew from their shirt pockets.

"Hello!" one of them said. They all stopped talking to stare at her.

"Hi." Making sure her own ID badge was showing, she stepped sideways to let them pass.

"How's it going?" another man asked.

"Fine, thank you."

She was tempted to run straight back to Rachel, but she forced herself to stay calm, relying on the assumption that the men had no idea what her real duties were. Sure enough, they walked past without further comment and Sydney stepped into the elevator.

Inside were buttons for twenty-three floors, including the lobby. Sydney hesitated, then pressed button 23.

ENTER SECURITY CODE appeared in red letters in the LCD display.

"Uh-oh," she said, quickly pressing 22 instead. The elevator began moving.

That could have cost me, she thought. Some elevators were programmed to lock down if a person tried to access a restricted floor without a security code. Luckily, this one was more forgiving. It took her to the twenty-second floor without further incident.

It's probably smarter not to start on Vincent's floor anyway, she thought as the doors opened on an empty hallway. *I'll just look around here.*

Sydney strolled casually down the hall, determined to blend in. The key was in the pacing—too slow and people would think she was lost, too fast and she might look nervous. She passed several large, luxurious offices, peeking through their open doorways. The first two were empty. In the third, a man hunched over a keyboard, his back turned toward the door. More empty offices followed until finally she happened upon a conference room and discovered where everyone was.

Raised voices floated into the hallway, stopping her before she reached the open door. Some sort of meeting was in progress. Sydney eased forward, listening.

"I'm just saying," a loud voice insisted. "At MicroCom they get four weeks' vacation *and* a 401k."

"Don't be dense," came the scornful reply. "I'm telling you: stock options."

"We ought to at least be able to choose our own health insurance. . . ."

Sydney backed away silently. This wasn't the kind of intel Wilson was looking for, although she couldn't help wondering if Owen Vincent knew what his employees talked about behind his back.

If SpaceSoft is having money problems, that could explain a lot, she thought, walking back down the hall the way she had come. *Whatever this missile guidance thing is, if Vincent could sell it quietly, under the table . . .*

Nearing the elevator, Sydney passed a closed door she hadn't noticed before. She glanced around to make sure no one was watching, then backed up and put her ear to the wood. No sound came from inside. Making a quick decision, she reached for the knob.

The room was a darkened library. A few rectangular tables near the doorway were strewn with books and papers, as if someone had recently been working there. Behind the tables were rows of tall freestanding bookshelves. A long bank of file cabinets occupied the distant back wall.

This looks like a good place to poke around, she thought, closing the door behind her and switching on a light. Moving quickly to the table, she began sorting through the papers lying there.

There were dozens of pages covered with handwritten equations and a roll of blueprints depicting some sort of engine. She was still trying to figure out whether the drawing was of a rocket engine when voices in the hallway made her freeze.

"I'm not going to worry about it anymore," someone said. "Owen always works these things out."

"Personally, I have more important things to do," came the deep-voiced reply. "If I don't finish those calcs by tomorrow . . ."

They're standing right outside the door! Sydney

realized. *And these are the calculations they're talking about.*

Abandoning the papers, she raced toward the back of the library, desperate to get away. The light was still on overhead, but there was nothing she could do about that now. Maybe they wouldn't notice her in the book stacks if she squeezed into a corner and held very, very still.

But what will Rachel do when I don't show up back downstairs?

Sydney cast about frantically for an escape route. The acoustic ceiling might be an option, but there wasn't time to climb up there and remove tiles. The room had no windows at all—besides, she was on the twenty-second floor.

And then, to her total amazement, she saw her out. In the very back corner of the room, nearly hidden in an alcove behind the last file cabinet, was a second door.

"I'll check back with you later," she heard the deep voice say, so clearly it could only mean the front door had been opened. Flying the final few feet to her escape, she grabbed the knob and pushed.

Locked.

No! she thought, slumping into a sitting position against the wood. She didn't have a lock pick, and she'd only be able to cower in the alcove for so long before Rachel started looking for her. She was going to have to bluff her way out.

Maybe she could say she'd come to fetch a book for someone. But who?

Or I could pretend to be looking *at the books. Gung-ho new hire. Overeager intern. I'll have to go with that.*

She was pushing up to her feet when the door she was leaning on suddenly opened, sending her sprawling backward. A hand grabbed her under one arm, simultaneously propping her up and pulling her through the opening. Something told her not to scream. Instead, she found her balance and twisted around, ready to fight.

"Noah!" she gasped as the door closed silently behind her, throwing his face into shadow. The room she'd tumbled into was big and dark, and without the light from the library, she could barely see him. "How did you find me here?" she whispered.

He put a finger to his lips and motioned for her to follow him. She crept along behind, tracking his silhouette, until he opened another door and let them into a small room lined with rickety metal shelves and janitorial supplies. A lightbulb glared overhead, giving Sydney her first clear look at her rescuer.

"Nice duds!" she said, laughing. "My knight in dirty coveralls!"

Noah was wearing a blue janitor's uniform with MICK embroidered in orange over its left pocket. A matching baseball cap covered his hair and shielded his face from any overhead cameras.

"Stylin', Mick," she added, still chuckling. "No wonder you didn't want to fill me in on your new career at SpaceSoft."

"Yeah? Well, maybe I don't think much of your wig, but *I'm* too professional to say so," Noah retorted, annoyed.

Sydney's hands went to her hair. "You don't like it?"

"That blond washes you out. Or maybe it's the blue eyes. I don't know; you look pale. Or wait," he added sarcastically, "maybe it's the fact that I just totally saved your butt. A screw-up like that could make anyone pale."

"How did you find me?" she asked sheepishly.

"I saw you on a security camera. They've got these janitor closets on every floor, and I've rigged a feed into an empty one a few floors down. You're lucky the security here is mostly for show, or it could have been someone else dragging you out of that room."

"I'd rather be lucky than good," Sydney joked, trying to lighten his mood.

"Great job, then—you're right on target. So here's what you're going to do now: Get back to your desk and start kissing up to Rachel. You'll learn a lot more gossiping with her than wandering around up here. Until we have a plan, recons like this are just crazy and pointless."

"Is that so?" she said, bristling.

"Look, I didn't mean—"

"I know what you meant."

He wasn't wrong, either; that was the worst part. She hated the way he always seemed to catch her messing up.

"How about dinner tonight?" he asked, trying to smooth things over. "That new Thai place on Flower's supposed to be good."

"I can't. My father's in town and I'm supposed to have dinner with him."

"Really?" Noah seemed amazed.

"What's so strange about that?"

"Nothing! Nothing, it's just . . ." He put on a teasing grin. "Maybe I don't like the idea of you going out with another guy."

Perfect, Sydney thought, her answering smile catching on her teeth. *I guess now's not the best time to mention Burke.*

* * *

By the time Sydney ditched her rental car and disguise at school and drove back downtown to the Union Hotel, she was running fifteen minutes late. Her palms were sweaty with anxiety, slipping on the wheel of her Mustang as she turned into the hotel drive. Her father was never late, and he wasn't going to appreciate her tardiness.

I could have been on time if I'd come dressed as Kristin Jarvis. She nearly laughed aloud imagining her straightlaced father's reaction to that blond wig and excess of makeup. *He'd freak out so bad I almost wish I'd done it.*

She would have gotten away with it, too, she realized. There wasn't a chance in the world he'd ever guess *why* she was dressed that way. But she couldn't risk blowing her mission just to give herself a thrill. Spying so close to home made it all the more important to keep her two lives separate.

A valet ran up to the Mustang, opening the driver's door before the car had fully stopped. Sydney handed over her keys, wishing she had time to park it herself. Her father was waiting, though, and she was already getting off on the wrong foot.

Not that there's a right foot, she thought, nervously checking her reflection in the hotel's glass entry doors.

Her hasty removal of Kristin's makeup had left her looking even more freshly scrubbed than usual, with only a little residual mascara and some pink gloss over her lips. Her hair was the worse for having spent the afternoon under a wig, but her black slacks and blazer were fresh from the cleaner. Taking a deep breath, Sydney walked through the automatic doors into the Union's lobby.

It was darker inside than out. She squeezed her eyes shut to adjust to the light, and when she opened them again her father had appeared on the opposite side of the room.

He looked exactly the same as always. A dark suit and tie had become his uniform over the years; she could barely remember him in anything else. His gray hair was short and combed with a slight wave over the forehead. His face was impassive—it was *always* impassive—and as she met his aloof gaze, she felt a sudden urge to run.

This is going to turn out badly, she thought, panicking. *It always turns out badly, and I'm going to wish I hadn't come.*

But she couldn't turn back now. He'd already seen her. She forced herself forward, her empty hands fluttering at her sides.

This part was always the worst, seeing him after a long absence. Part of her wanted to hug him, or at least shake hands, but her body wouldn't let her. The distance between them just seemed too vast.

Not that he was rushing toward her with open arms. Jack Bristow stood where he was, letting her come to him.

She covered the final few feet, stopping awkwardly at arm's length. He hadn't mentioned her lateness, so maybe this was a good start after all. She searched his face for a sign.

"Hi, Dad," she ventured at last. "Sorry I'm late. I got here as soon as I could."

Jack twitched his head slightly. Annoyance? Dismissal? Forgiveness? She didn't have a clue.

"Hello, Sydney," he said coolly.

4

"SPACESOFT TECHNOLOGIES. THIS IS
Ssss—Kristin," Sydney said into the phone, so consumed by her personal problems that she almost made a stupid mistake.

"Give me Bob McKee," a voice demanded on the other end. "Tell him it's Roger. He'll know why."

"Just a minute, sir," she said, pressing a button. The light went dead—she'd lost him—and the next word to escape her lips made her glad no one else was in SST's lobby.

"Rachel is going to kill me," she groaned.

After two more hours of training that Tuesday, Sydney's new supervisor had decided she was finally competent to handle the switchboard alone, but over the past ten minutes, Sydney had dropped three calls and transferred two to the wrong people. She was already counting the seconds until Rachel came back from her break.

This is harder than it looks, she thought. *Especially when your head's not in the game.*

She couldn't concentrate on the switchboard, couldn't concentrate on her mission, couldn't even rouse herself enough to wonder whether Noah was in the building. All she could think about was dinner with her father the night before—and how horribly awkward it had been.

Considering how long he'd been away, they should have been able to find *something* to talk about. She'd done her best to start a conversation about South America. But all she'd gotten back from him were dry recitations of facts—menus, customs, populations, elevations.

Elevations! she thought as the phone rang again. *What kind of social misfit goes to exotic foreign cities and remembers their elevations?*

"SpaceSoft Technologies," she said into the phone. "This is Kristin."

"You just hung up on me, Kristin," a testy voice informed her. "How about transferring me to Bob McKee this time?"

"Right. I'm so sorry. If you could just hold for a second—"

"I don't want to hold."

Another line started ringing.

"All right. I'm transferring you. It's just that I have to put you on hold to ring you through to Mr. McKee. Five seconds, I promise."

"I'll be counting."

She put the caller on hold and picked up the second line. "SpaceSoft Technologies. This is Kristin."

"Yes. Uh . . . I was wondering . . ."

Across the lobby, Sydney saw the front door open. A scruffy-looking young guy wearing shorts and flip-flops walked in, his layered sun-bleached hair the perfect complement to his surf shop T-shirt.

". . . um," the caller continued. "Do you have any openings?"

"What kind of openings?" she asked, tracking Scruffy's progress over the immaculately polished black floor.

"Like, say . . . for jobs?"

"I'm not sure. I'll have to put you on hold."

Scruffy reached the desk just as Sydney pressed the Hold button.

"Hey. How's it going?" he asked.

She held up her left index finger, dialing Bob McKee's extension with her right. Luckily, he picked up quickly.

"Mr. McKee? You have a phone call," she said all in a rush. The second line was still on hold, and a third light had just started blinking.

"Who is it?" he asked.

"It's . . . I forgot," Sydney admitted miserably. "But he said you know him."

"Who are *you*?"

"Kristin Jarvis. I'm new, and I'm really sorry. Do you want me to ask his name again?" Her tone pleaded for mercy.

"No, put him through. Just pay more attention next time."

"I will," Sydney promised gratefully, transferring the line.

"I want—" Scruffy tried again.

"One second." Sydney cut him off. "Just let me get these phones."

She transferred the job hunter from hold to Human Resources. The new caller wanted driving directions to SST from somewhere in Orange County.

"I'll have to ask you to hold," Sydney said, pressing the button. The light on the switchboard went dead.

"Oh *no*!" she exclaimed. "Did they just hang up on *me*? I think they hung up on me." She put a hand to her aching head. "At least I really hope so."

Scruffy leaned forward across the counter and flashed an ingratiating smile. "I can't imagine anyone hanging up on you."

"Then you don't have much of an imagination," she said, ignoring his attempt to flirt. "What can I help you with?"

"I was wondering if you have anything for me. Behind the desk, I mean."

"Like a package?" Sydney glanced around her work area, confused. Rachel hadn't said anything about a package to be picked up.

"A roll of plans. They could be wrapped in brown paper."

From where she was standing, she could see the plans clearly, leaning against the inside of the counter. They had been tantalizing her ever since she'd come on shift and noticed the tag addressed to Mr. Vincent attached to their brown wrapping, but she hadn't been able to sneak a look yet. She shook her head at Scruffy.

"Sorry. Not unless you're Owen Vincent."

Scruffy's face lit up. "As a matter of fact . . ."

"Yeah, right. Don't even try it. I've seen the man's picture, and you're not him."

"The picture behind the fountain? In the atrium?" he asked, pointing in exactly the right direction.

"Yes," Sydney said cautiously.

"What a relief! I'd have to shoot myself if I looked like that. If I looked like that all the time, I mean."

"That's not you," she repeated, but she was suddenly a lot less sure. Part of her brain was busy imagining Scruffy with a shave, a crew cut, and a really boring tie—and the picture in her head lined up a little too closely with the one on the bulletin board. "I mean, you're so much younger," she added desperately.

"Suits age a guy—which is why I try not to wear them. Funerals and contract signings are the only time I look like that stiff in my picture. I mean, why pay a marketing department if they're not going to wear the uncomfortable clothes, go to the boring meetings, and do whatever else I don't want to do?"

There was no further doubt in her mind. This scruffy, laid-back guy was Owen Vincent.

"I'm so sorry!" Sydney said, knowing she'd be

even sorrier if Vincent fired her. "It's just that I'm new, and the phone's been ringing off the hook, and . . . I swear it won't happen again."

Owen waved off her apology. "Not a problem. I like it when people don't recognize me."

"Really? Why is that?" she asked, hoping for some useful intel.

But Vincent just gave her a flirty smile. "Maybe sometimes I get tired of being a software nerd. A guy likes to have options."

Sydney was trying to decide whether to flirt back when Rachel walked into the lobby, loaded down with mail.

"Hi, Owen," she said. "Somebody dropped off some plans for you."

"I know. Kristin was just getting them for me."

Rachel dropped the mail on the counter next to Sydney. "How were the waves?"

"Small and stinky," he replied. "Hardly worth getting wet."

Sydney handed him his package.

"Thanks, Kristin. Catch you later." With a parting wink, he sauntered off in the direction of the elevators, his flip-flops slapping time.

"I can't believe it," Sydney groaned, slumping against the counter. "Why didn't you *tell* me?"

"Tell you what?" Rachel asked.

"That Mr. Vincent was coming in, and that—oh, yeah—he's a total surf rat!"

Rachel laughed. "Nothing that drastic. He's just . . . Owen. Listen, how about leaving now and taking that mail to the post office? The letters'll get there a day sooner and you'll get off a half hour early."

"Okay."

She had already lost her chance to see the plans. Besides, with the kind of day she'd been having, it was safer to get out before she ruined anything else. Gathering up the mail, Sydney beat a quick retreat to the parking lot.

She was waiting at the second traffic light before it occurred to her there might be spying opportunities right in her lap. Pulling to the curb, she flipped through the envelopes, some white, some manila. A stiff manila one addressed to the FBI immediately caught her eye.

Could it be?

It didn't seem likely she'd get that lucky, but she ripped the envelope open, not even trying to be sly. Two fingerprint cards fell into her lap, one for Kristin Jarvis and one for Mick LaMonte.

So much for SST security, she thought, feeling a little better as she tossed them onto the car's floor mats. *If only the rest of my life were so easy!*

* * *

"Fantastic progress!" Wilson said when she checked in at headquarters. "It's better you *didn't* recognize Vincent. Now he thinks you're just some green young thing to hit on."

"That could be useful," Sydney agreed, her confidence back on the rise. Despite her problems with the switchboard, she had still made contact with the primary target of SD-6's investigation— not to mention snagged both her own and Noah's fingerprint cards.

Not bad for an afternoon's work.

Wilson continued flipping through SpaceSoft's mail, looking for other items of interest. "What have you got going tomorrow?" he asked.

"Well, classes, of course. And my shift at SST. Then I'm supposed to meet someone for dinner."

She didn't feel like telling Wilson the "someone" was her father. If he started asking questions about her family, they could be there all night. And she was suddenly so tired. . . .

"Plus I've still got a load of studying to catch up on from Hawaii, and I wouldn't mind getting to bed early for once, either."

Wilson nodded, still busy with the mail. "I get

the hint. I'll try not to work you to death." He looked up abruptly. "I mean—I didn't mean . . ."

Sydney smiled at his stricken expression. "Thanks."

"Good," he said, smiling back.

For just a second, she imagined tucking her head against Wilson's broad shoulder and falling fast asleep. She'd be safe there. She'd be warm and welcome. In so many ways, Wilson was more of a father to her than Jack would ever be.

"I want you to go see Graham," he said. "If Vincent talks to you again, let's get it on tape."

"Okay," she said, perking up.

She had used Graham's gadgets in Paris, but she had never actually met SD-6's high-tech genius. Noah knew him, though, and had raved about how smart he was.

Wilson dialed an extension on his speaker phone.

"Hello?" answered a muffled voice.

"Graham? This is Reg Wilson."

Sydney heard a crash that could have been a chair falling over. A moment later, Graham came back on the line, his voice considerably more clear. "Hello, sir!"

Wilson shook his head for Sydney's benefit.

"Graham, I've got Sydney Bristow in my office, and she needs some gear for the SST mission. How about coming in here and getting her?"

"Sure!" he said eagerly. "Sure, I'll be right there."

Wilson hung up the phone. "I don't know why these gadget guys are always so odd, but Graham's one of the best. Don't let his lack of social skills fool you."

Before Sydney could reply, Graham burst into the office, his arms windmilling backward to keep him from sliding into Wilson's big desk.

"Hi! Hi, sir! Here I am."

"So I see," Wilson said dryly. "Graham, this is Sydney. How about showing her where you work?"

"Yeah! That'd be great."

"See you later," Wilson told her with a wink.

The next thing Sydney knew, she was following Graham through a maze of back hallways into a room heaped high with disemboweled computers, recycled electronic components, wires, microphones, bugs, pliers, magnifying glasses, soldering irons, and at least five monitors, all of which were on. A battered swivel chair lay on its back in the middle of this chaos, and Graham rushed to set it on its wheels, motioning for her to sit down.

"Sorry about the mess," he said anxiously. "I

was just . . . You don't want to lean too far back in that chair."

"Okay," Sydney said, stifling a smile as she took the seat.

Graham rubbed his hands together. "So. You're on surveillance at SpaceSoft Technologies."

"Yep."

He seemed to expect more, but she had no idea what he wanted to hear.

"I applied there once," he said at last. "When I first got out of college. Well, actually twice. Three times, if you count that internship."

"You were an intern there too?"

"Actually . . . no. That place is harder to crack than the CIA." He gestured around him. "Obviously, right? But, no. It's not that I'm not happy here. I just never figured out . . . I mean, I'm *good* at what I do."

"Everyone says you're the best," Sydney reassured him.

"Really?" Graham pulled himself up to full height. "Because I am pretty good."

"So what do you have for me? Wilson wants me to record my conversations with Owen Vincent."

"He does? Okay. I have just the thing." Graham rooted around on a cluttered tabletop and came up with a pen.

"Just a pen, right?" he asked, holding it up for her inspection. "It looks like a pen, writes like a pen." He pulled off the cap and mimed writing in the air. "But anytime the nib is extended, it's a digital recorder. *Plus,* it's a transmitter. You can leave it in someone's office and hear what's being said with this earpiece."

He handed her a tiny, flesh-colored lump that he shook out of the pen cap. "Totally invisible once you have it in. Oh, and there's an eraser!"

Turning to a desk, he opened a drawer and removed a polygonal pink eraser. "Remember these from grade school? Don't you love the way they smell?" He held it up to his nose and took a big whiff. "But this one has a directional microphone inside. Point it at what you want to hear, and it magnifies sound like a giant boom mike. You can leave it lying out somewhere, but it's really cool for listening through walls. Hold it to a wall, like this, and you can totally hear what's going on in the next room—it feeds right to your earpiece. *Plus,* it links to the pen, so you can record whatever you want."

"That'll work," Sydney said, reaching for the pen and eraser. Given Graham's reputation for genius, she was a little disappointed that his offerings were so pedestrian, but they were exactly the types of things people would expect to see in an office. She could use them right in the open without arousing suspicion.

"I know what you're thinking," he said. "Not very exciting, right?"

"No," Sydney lied. "They're great."

"No, you're right," he said, shoulders slumping. "They're the right tools for the job, but they're not very sexy." All of a sudden his face lit up. "Oh, I have something for you! Something *very* cool."

Turning to a file cabinet piled to the ceiling with junk, Graham opened a drawer and extracted a small white envelope. He shook something from it into his upturned palm and proudly extended his hand to Sydney. She had to look twice to see the tiny iridescent oblong, an eighth the size of a grain of rice, resting in his lifeline.

"What is that?" she asked.

"Edible transmitter," he said, beaming. "You put this in Mr. Vincent's coffee, and its density keeps it floating right in the middle of the liquid. The coating reflects surrounding colors, making it almost invisible. He swallows it, none the wiser. Then you can listen to him on your earpiece *and* record him on your pen. You'll get every word he says—so long as you're both in the building."

"Wait. We have to be in the SST building?"

"Or within a hundred yards of each other somewhere else," Graham said, his smile dimming slightly. "That's the only drawback with all three of these devices: I had to scale back the signals to avoid detection during scans. SST has got to have *somebody* sweeping for bugs. I mean, I hope they do. Unless they're stupid. Which, now that I'm thinking about it, would explain a lot. . . ."

A faraway look entered his eyes as he considered that pleasant possibility.

"Anyway," he said abruptly, snapping back to the present, "once Vincent swallows this, you're golden until it passes out of his system. Twenty, thirty hours—maybe longer."

"That's pretty vague," she protested. "Can't you narrow it down?"

Graham shrugged. "Depends how regular Vincent is. When you're serving his coffee, steer him away from the bran muffins."

"Right," she said, sorry she'd asked.

"Which reminds me, you might get some background noise," he continued matter-of-factly. "Stomach acid, gas, that type of thing. And then, of course, the device will eventually pass. . . ."

"Super," Sydney said weakly.

She could only hope she wouldn't be listening then.

By the time Sydney climbed the last flight of stairs to her dorm room, she was ready to collapse. The past three days had been exhausting; all she wanted to do was sleep and forget about them.

Put in two good hours with the books and then you can go to bed early, she promised herself, walking up to her room. *Maybe Francie will want to split a pizza before we crash.*

She opened her door hopefully, looking forward to finally spending some time with her best friend, but the scene inside stopped her dead in her tracks.

Three girls were crammed into her small room, surrounded by shopping bags and tissue paper. Francie sprawled diagonally across her twin bed, another girl lounged on the floor, and a total stranger had commandeered Sydney's bed, her back propped up with Sydney's pillows. The CD player was blaring, but no one seemed to be listening to the music. Instead, the girls were talking animatedly among themselves, breaking off their conversation when Francie caught sight of Sydney.

"Hey, Syd. There you are," she said, turning down the stereo. "You're home early."

"Not really."

Between her shift at SST, her visits with Wilson

and Graham, and ditching her Kristin Jarvis disguise, she was over an hour later than she'd be on a normal day at the "bank."

"No? I guess I didn't notice." Francie shrugged, turning her attention back to her guests.

"*Anyway*," the girl on the floor said, completely ignoring Sydney. "We *have* to go tomorrow. If there's any chance he'll be working again . . ."

"Oh! Oh!" The one on Sydney's bed cut in. "One, two—"

"*Free!*" all of them cried together, dissolving into uncontrollable laughter.

Sydney smiled uneasily. She wanted to be friendly, but she had no idea what they were talking about. Not only that, but there was nowhere good left to sit. Picking her way through the mess on the floor, she set her backpack on her desk and managed to pull her chair out far enough to squeeze into it sideways, twisting around to see Francie and her new friends. All three girls were wearing cropped baby blue T-shirts—identical baby blue T-shirts, with UCLA in gold letters across their chests. They looked like a sorority.

A sorority of three.

"I was thinking maybe we could call for a pizza," Sydney said when the giggles died down.

She ventured a smile at the girl on her bed. "If you guys are staying, we could get two."

"We already ate," the girl replied, pummeling one of Sydney's pillows to make it more comfortable.

"Sorry," Francie added. "I didn't know you'd want pizza."

"It doesn't matter. I'm not that hungry," Sydney lied, ignoring her growling stomach.

"There's some caramel corn in one of these bags," Francie offered, pointing without getting up. "I couldn't finish it all."

"You went shopping again, huh?"

The girl on the floor gave Sydney a disbelieving look. "We didn't whip up a batch of caramel in here."

"No. Right." Sydney shifted her weight uncomfortably. "I'm sorry. I didn't get your name."

"Didn't I introduce everyone?" Francie roused herself a little. "This is Shauna and Carly," she said, pointing to the floor and Sydney's bed, respectively. "And this is my roommate, Sydney."

Roommate? Sydney caught her breath, hurt.

"So are we going?" Shauna demanded, looking from Francie to Carly. "We are, right? We *have* to."

"I'll tell you what we should do," Carly said, rolling onto her side. Her bare feet scrabbled on Sydney's bedspread, tangling it into a lump. "Operation Ego."

"More like Operation Afro," Francie said. "Puh-lease!"

They all started laughing hysterically, not the least bit concerned that Sydney didn't get the joke.

"You're bad!" said Shauna, reaching up to slap Francie's leg.

"What's bad is that guy's hair!" Carly gasped between giggles.

"I have to study," Sydney blurted out.

Francie gave her a startled look. "Okay. Go ahead."

Sydney glanced meaningfully around the room. Francie just stared blankly.

"In the library," Sydney said at last, rising to her feet and slinging her backpack over one shoulder. Every cell in her body protested, crying out for a shower, a pizza, and bed. But there was no way she'd ever get any of that with Shauna and Carly around.

Besides, she obviously wasn't welcome.

"See you later," Francie said as Sydney headed out.

Sydney opened the door, then stopped, turning to face her best friend. "See you later. Roomie."

Francie didn't flinch. She didn't even get it.

"So, what are we wearing tomorrow?" Sydney heard Carly ask as she closed the door.

To: jack.bristow@credit-dauphine.com

From: reginald.wilson@credit-dauphine.com

Subject: Sydney

Received your message and am distressed to hear you didn't know Sydney was recruited. Arvin implied you were in the loop. You must realize he'd have activated her with or without me, but as her handler I've done my best to keep her out of harm's way. She's an exceptional girl, Jack. You must be very proud.

Reg

5

"I'M NOT SURE WHY you'd volunteer for this," Rachel said, pushing her glasses up her small nose, "but I love you for it."

She and Sydney were alone in the SpaceSoft lobby, confronting a pile of mail to be processed, an unusually active switchboard, and a new "filler" project involving typing individualized labels for three hundred folders.

"No problem," Sydney replied. "I'd much rather pass around coffee and sandwiches than tackle those phones again. I was a waitress once, you know." No need to mention she'd been fired her first day.

"Weren't we all?" Rachel said with a sigh. "Okay, you know how to find your way back to the main conference room. The food's already in there. All you have to do is make the coffee and—"

"Completely under control," Sydney assured her. "Don't worry. I'm on it."

"I'm not *worried*," Rachel said. "It's just that these client meetings are a pretty big deal, and Owen can be surprisingly particular if he thinks—"

The telephone rang, then rang again, a cascade of blinking lights.

"Why?" Rachel asked the ceiling. "Why does it always have to be five lines at once?"

"I'll just go get started," Sydney said quickly.

Rachel switched on her headset. "SpaceSoft Technologies. This is Rachel speaking. . . ."

Sydney had to force herself not to skip as she escaped down a series of back hallways to SST's most deluxe conference room. Rachel had taken her there in a panic just fifteen minutes earlier, which was when Sydney had first learned of the major client meeting Owen Vincent was holding that Wednesday afternoon.

Talk about timing! she thought, letting one

hand stray to the pocket of her linen pants, where Graham's tiny edible bug was hidden in a wad of Kleenex. The receiver was already in her ear. *I could have waited weeks for a chance like this!*

She strode into the empty conference room, determined to take full advantage of the opportunity.

A double-long burled hardwood table dominated the center of the oblong room. The curved walls were covered with dark red silk, and plush silver carpeting snuffed the sound of her footsteps as she entered. The ornately carved ceiling likewise seemed to have acoustic properties. The entire room was so quiet she could suddenly hear herself breathing.

Soundproofing. But that's not a problem since I plan to eavesdrop from inside, she thought, touching her pocket again. *Way inside.*

At one curved end of the room, a white screen had been set up in preparation for some sort of presentation. Sydney headed toward the built-in bar at the other end, where two pink bakery boxes and an array of deli sandwiches waited beside a sleek black coffeemaker.

Coffee first, she thought, focusing on the reason she'd volunteered to waitress in the first place.

Fifteen minutes later, when Rachel ushered the first clients into the meeting room, the steam from a fresh pot of coffee perfumed the air, the sandwiches were arranged on two platters, and a dozen assorted gourmet pastries waited on individual dessert plates. Sydney had already put sandwich plates and mugs in front of twelve black leather chairs, and now she stood nervously to one side, waiting to serve the food and coffee.

Especially the coffee.

"Have a seat, gentlemen," Rachel said, shepherding her charges to the part of the table Sydney had prepared. "Mr. Vincent will join you soon."

She flashed Sydney a quick thumbs-up before exiting again. A moment later, Owen entered the room, offering a pained smile when he caught her eyeing his suit and fresh haircut.

"I know," he mouthed silently, shrugging to indicate that the situation had been out of his hands.

Sydney found herself smiling back, actually pitying him.

He hadn't opted for his brochure crew cut this time, but his hair was inches shorter than before, well above his stiff white collar, and all of the sun streaks were gone. His suit was gray, his shoes shiny black, his tie a masterpiece of bland conformity. He held his briefcase like a prop, abandoning it on the floor as he began greeting his guests.

"Hello, Mac," he said, reaching to shake a

hand. "Anthony, glad you could make it." The atmosphere was formal, but the men all seemed to know each other, leaving Sydney to deduce who they were without the benefit of introductions.

Rachel reappeared with another group, this one including two women. Her brown eyes turned wistful as she watched them take seats at the table, but she didn't hesitate long, stopping only to whisper to Sydney, "Just three more, and they're here all the time, so I'll send them in on their own. Start serving the sandwiches."

"Okay," Sydney whispered back, springing into action.

The other three clients arrived in short order, and for a while, the conference room sounded more like a diner than a high-tech business meeting. Sydney carried the sandwich trays around, using the opportunity to memorize faces. Nine of the clients were men, two women, and Vincent made it an even dozen. None of them mentioned the reason they'd come; instead, talk revolved around the unseasonably hot weather and whether it would continue into summer. No one paid attention as Sydney worked the edible bug out of her pocket and into the palm of her left hand. She was just an invisible waitress.

"Coffee?" she asked brightly, beginning to make her first round with the pot. "Coffee?"

She lifted each cup to fill it, establishing a pattern so Vincent wouldn't think twice when she handled his. Everything went perfectly as she worked her way up the table, her pulse getting faster with every step. She was reaching for Vincent's cup, relieved to see that her hand was still steady, when disaster struck.

"No thanks," he said quickly, covering his cup with his hand. "I never drink the stuff."

"But . . . but . . . you have to drink something," she protested. "I could get you some tea. . . ."

"There's bottled water in the refrigerator. Bring out a few, in case anyone else wants one."

Sydney nodded, abandoning the remaining empty coffee cups in her hurry to fetch the water.

Back at the bar, she yanked the paneled minifridge open, retrieving three bottles of Evian. She had planned to open one and drop the bug inside with her back still to Vincent, but now she hesitated, afraid the device might be visible through the clear plastic. Or what if it didn't float right in water? The density of coffee couldn't be significantly different . . . but did she need to factor in temperature?

"Kristin?" Vincent called behind her. "Is there a problem?"

"No! No problem," she said, straightening up. She hurried back to the table, setting down two bottles and holding the third out to Vincent. "Is this okay?"

"Looks like water to me," he said, reaching for the bottle.

She pulled it back. "I'll open it for you. Or how about a cup?" If she could pour the water into something that wasn't transparent . . .

"No, just give it here. I like the bottle."

Sydney froze, stymied. Vincent raised an eyebrow at her. She handed the bottle over, unopened.

"Can I get some coffee now?" one of the clients she'd skipped before asked.

"Huh? Oh. Sure."

For the next ten minutes Sydney hovered around the table, refilling cups, removing plates, and obsessing about her missed opportunity. Who knew when she'd be this close again?

She cruised slowly past Owen's chair, wondering if she could drop the bug down his shirt collar. She wouldn't get more than a few hours of surveillance that way, but maybe she'd get enough. At least she'd hear the meeting. Her hand strayed toward his neck. Closer, closer . . .

"Kristin?" he said, making her jump. He looked over his shoulder, right into her fake blue eyes. "How about that dessert? The sooner it's on the table, the sooner we can start our meeting and you can get back to Rachel."

"Of course." Palming the bug again, Sydney headed off to fetch the desserts.

"I'll have the chocolate," one of the women said. Sydney handed it over, easily finding takers for the others she held as well.

"Did they send my carrot cake?" Vincent asked. "The one with the cream cheese frosting?"

The carrot cake he'd asked for was a gooey slice slathered in thick white icing with piped orange decorations. Sydney had already picked it up when inspiration struck. The tiny bug was still in her hand, and there was no way Vincent would see it tucked down in all that icing. Most likely he'd swallow it without a clue. If the worst happened, and he bit down on the device, he'd think it was a nut. Either way, she wouldn't get caught. Quickly, before she could second-guess herself, Sydney dropped the bug onto the cake and pushed it into the frosting. Then, grabbing two more selections, she returned to the table and set the cake in front of Vincent.

"Mmm. That looks good," a man sitting a few

chairs away remarked enviously, eyeing the carrot cake.

"Here," Vincent said, sliding his untouched cake down the table.

Sydney's stomach dropped to her feet.

"I couldn't." The client pushed it back.

"This coconut cake looks great!" Sydney said, rushing in while she had the chance. She put it in front of the client, turning the plate to show its icing. "They're very similar. Really."

"Then I'll eat it," said Vincent, motioning for the man to switch with him. "It doesn't matter to me."

"Well, if you're sure . . ."

Sydney held her breath. *No, no, no, no . . .*

"Of course. I can get that carrot cake anytime," Vincent said, sliding it back over and snagging the other plate. "Besides, you're my guest."

"Thank you," the client said, pleased. He picked up a fork, preparing to plunge in.

"Whoops!" Sydney cried in a panic. "I think I see something dirty on that plate! Let me take it and get you a clean one."

She lunged for the dessert, ignoring the heads swiveling her way. Her fingers touched china . . . then lost it again as the client pulled the plate from her grasp.

"This is *fine*," he said, giving her an annoyed

look. "I don't see a thing." Aiming his fork again, he took a huge bite of the cake, making his point irrefutable.

"Thanks, Kristin." Vincent's tone had gone ice cold. "Now leave us to our business."

* * *

All the way across campus, rushing from the gym to her dorm, Sydney tortured herself with her mistake at SST.

Vincent's client had swallowed Graham's high-tech bug. Worse, Vincent had given her a truly nasty look as she'd left the conference room. Had she tipped him off somehow? Did he suspect her of spying, or just incompetence?

If it's incompetence, no worries, she told herself miserably. *The incompetence part is true.*

She had spent the remainder of her afternoon at SpaceSoft trying to pick up the signal from the bug inside the client, but he wasn't saying much, and most of the other voices were too far away to make out. She'd recorded the meeting on her pen anyway, in case Graham could enhance the transmission enough to make sense, but she didn't have a lot of hope. At least Rachel had been able to give her the name of her unintended victim: Robert Armstrong.

"He's new in town. Independent contractor. I'm not too sure what his deal is," Rachel had told her, sticking labels to folders at a furious pace. "But," she'd added with an ill-concealed grin, "so far as I know, the future of SpaceSoft Technologies doesn't hang on him getting a clean plate."

"I should have left it alone," Sydney had said, groaning. "I just wanted everything to be perfect. You said Mr. Vincent can be particular."

"True. But you have to know what he's particular about. Making a scene in front of a client is *huge*—much worse than a smudged plate."

"I figured that out," she'd said miserably.

"It's not like you offended someone important," Rachel had reassured her. "Owen and Robert met at some lame association picnic. Besides, my bet is that Robert's only posing as a consultant until he can hit Owen up for a real job. Forget about it. Honestly."

But the debacle in the conference room was all Sydney could think about. She had driven from SST to the school gym in a haze, stripping off her Kristin wig and clothes in a toilet stall and stashing them in her locker. A couple of makeup-removing cloths later and she was Sydney again, but her mind was still far away as she hurried to the dorm to change clothes once more, this time for dinner with her father. She would have loved to cancel, but she couldn't think of an excuse that wouldn't create worse problems than simply showing up.

Suffer now or suffer later. Besides, he'll be gone again soon. These bouts of togetherness never last.

Although Jack hadn't actually told her yet how long he'd be in town this time. He was only taking a break from his tour of South America—that much she'd deduced—but when he'd be going back to work was anybody's guess.

Soon, I hope. She just didn't know how many more awkward, cold, emotionally draining evenings she could stand while everything else in her life was so—

"Sydney?"

She had been dodging her fellow pedestrians without thinking, almost without seeing, so Burke nearly got mown over by stepping out in front of her.

"Burke!" she exclaimed, stopping just in time. "Sorry. My brain was somewhere else."

"Yeah. I could practically hear you thinking from all the way over there." He pointed to a wire-topped table a few feet away, where an open book and a cup of coffee sat abandoned. "You just getting back from work?"

"Yeah. It was a nightmare. I mean, we've got all

these projects. . . ." She blinked a few times, trying to reorient herself to the set of lies that comprised her "normal" life.

"Your eyes . . . they're blue!"

Sydney's heart nearly stopped. In her rush to leave the gym, she'd forgotten to take out Kristin's contacts.

"Well, I just thought . . . I mean, as an experiment . . . ," she fumbled.

"You're so beautiful," he said, laying his hands on her cheeks and staring more deeply into her eyes.

"Really?" she said, relieved. "You like them?"

"I hate them. Which only proves my point."

"I . . . huh?"

"If you still look this good with those ridiculous things in your eyes, imagine how gorgeous you are without them."

He had caught her off guard. The blood rushed to her face. She could see that he meant what he'd said, and his eyes were suddenly full of other things too—things she wasn't sure she was ready to hear.

"You're not bad yourself," she joked uneasily.

"Have dinner with me tonight."

"I can't. I have . . . that history quiz Friday, remember? And a paper due next week. And . . . a bunch of other stuff."

She might have told him about Jack, but she

didn't have the time. The nature of her relationship with her father wasn't a two-second explanation to be tossed off in the middle of campus. It was more like a Russian novel; to understand it required patience, a box of tissues, and several vodka shooters.

"I have to go," she said, trying not to notice how sad he looked. "I'm sorry."

She stretched up on her toes, dropping a kiss on his lips, but Burke didn't perk up the way she had hoped.

"When will I see you?" he asked. "I mean, *really* see you. When are you going to have time for me?"

"Soon," she promised, feeling awful and guilty and probably wrong. He was so sweet . . . and she was such a liar. "Just let me get through finals, okay?"

He held her eyes a moment longer, then reluctantly let her go.

"Don't forget," he whispered, touching the tip of her nose. "I'm going to hold you to that."

* * *

"I thought the food here would be more authentic," Jack remarked, prodding a half-eaten chile relleno with his fork. "This is tourist fare."

"Not on Olvera Street!" Sydney exclaimed, pretending shock. She knew she was being obnoxious, but his choice of dinner location was incomprehensible to her. The single long block on which their restaurant was located was the oldest, most historic spot in downtown Los Angeles, but it was also a magnet for tourists in search of tacos, T-shirts, and strolling mariachis. "Didn't you get enough Mexican food in South America?"

"Perhaps next quarter you'll take geography," he said, pushing his plate away. "It doesn't matter; I'm full. How about you? Flan?"

"No, thanks."

Sydney stared at her father across their mosaic-topped table for two, trying to read his mind. Ever since they'd met up that evening, he'd seemed determined to treat her as younger than she was, and she couldn't figure out why. The aggressively festive restaurant, the fuss he'd made when he hadn't heard the "virgin" in her margarita order, his constant references to school . . .

I'm surprised he didn't ask the waitress for a booster seat.

The worst part was that the younger he treated her, the younger she acted. She could practically feel herself regressing.

"Well, if we're done here, let's go outside while

the shops are still open," he said. "Maybe one of them has something you'll want."

Like a pony?

Jack dropped a tip on the table and the two of them made their way to the cashier. Sydney stood off to one side while her father paid their bill, wondering what she was so mad about. After all, she had wanted his attention. So why wasn't she happy now that he was finally making an effort?

Because he still doesn't see me, she realized. *He's lost in some fantasy world where he's a dutiful dad and I'm a little girl. He doesn't know me at all.*

Outside the restaurant, the narrow pedestrian street was deep in evening shade, but the sun hadn't yet disappeared. Sydney followed her father past a burbling, triple-tiered fountain and along a row of shops with wares spilling onto the pavement, creating the illusion of stalls in an open-air market. She saw clothing, piñatas, woven blankets, huaraches, and, peering into the stores' dim interiors, brightly painted ceramics, candles, and glassware.

"What are you doing this summer?" Jack asked, falling back to walk at her side.

Sydney shrugged. "I'd like to get through finals before I worry about summer."

"But afterwards," he persisted. "Any plans?"

"I don't know. Whatever."

"I see. And what, exactly, does 'whatever' consist of?"

He wasn't going to take the hint, and his questions were making her squirm. There was no doubt in her mind that Wilson would plan her entire summer. But what could she tell her father?

"The bank has a filing backlog," she said. "If I help get them caught up, they might let me start teller training."

Jack nodded thoughtfully. "I admire your initiative, but it's misplaced."

"What's that supposed to mean?"

"You're nineteen. You're an *English* major, Sydney. Where are you going at Credit Dauphine? What I mean to ask is, what are your long-term plans there?"

The sudden intensity of his gaze made Sydney feel weak in the knees.

He knows, she thought. *He knows about SD-6.*

Then reality kicked in.

There was no way her stodgy father could have a clue about her involvement with the CIA. He was only being parental. Or attempting to be, anyway.

"Some people might be glad their kid was trying to earn her own way," she said. "I remember a spending-cash shortage before I started my job."

Her father's thin lips pressed into a line. He seemed about to snap out a retort.

"Did you know your school offers a summer session in London?" he asked instead. "You could be attending an English university, studying British literature with British professors. Wouldn't that be more valuable than filing paperwork at the bank?"

"Valuable to whom?" she asked sullenly.

Jack gave her an exasperated look. "I'm trying to help you, Sydney! If you want to go to London, I'm more than happy to pay."

The most annoying part was, she *did* want to go. She'd heard about the summer-abroad program, but hadn't let herself even consider participating. Money wasn't the problem; she just couldn't be gone that long. Not with Wilson counting on her . . .

"I'd like to go, but not this year," she said at last. "The bank needs me."

"The bank does *not* need you—that's my point. Quit your job and go to London."

"Why don't you quit *your* job?" she retorted, sounding exactly as childish as he obviously thought she was. "I suppose the airplanes of the world would fall out of the sky if you weren't the one who sold their parts."

Jack looked skyward, pained. "Now you're just being—"

"What? What am I being?" she challenged. "What makes your job more important than mine?"

"You don't know anything about my job."

"I know it's kept you out of my life! You go where you want, do what you want, and only see me when you want."

"You can't honestly believe that."

"No," she said spitefully. "You probably *never* want to see me. You only show up when you think you have to."

"That's not true."

"Then tell me, Dad, what goes on at Jennings Aerospace that's more important than raising your own daughter?"

Her voice had been rising by degrees, and now she was practically shouting. Jack glanced self-consciously around the crowded plaza.

"I'm not going to discuss this here," he said in a low voice. "I didn't *have* to come to L.A. this week."

"So why did you?"

"I don't know anymore."

"That makes two of us!"

She could feel the tears about to burst free, but that only made her more angry. She stood there glaring, out of words, then abruptly turned and ran across the plaza. There was music playing and people were laughing, but all Sydney heard were her own ragged breaths and the sound of her rapid footfalls. She didn't glance back once until she'd reached a grassy park.

Jack hadn't followed her. She hadn't expected him to.

He's gone, she realized, torn. *No way would he stick around town after that.*

Her father hated emotional outbursts. He hated emotion of any sort.

He's gone, she thought again. *Good riddance!*

6

"YOU'RE GOING TO MISS class," Francie warned.

A flying pillow hit Sydney's head, launched from across the room.

"It's early," Sydney complained, opening her eyes and squinting into the morning light. Francie was already up and dressed, her backpack slung over one shoulder. "Hey, what time is it?"

"It's exactly half an hour since you beat your alarm clock into submission. If that thing doesn't work tomorrow, you have only yourself to blame."

"Oh." She did vaguely remember knocking something across the room. "I'm just so tired."

"I'm not surprised. You were out awfully late with your father. I thought you were only having dinner."

"Ugh. Don't remind me."

Forcing herself to sit up, Sydney swung her bare feet to the floor. "We got in this huge fight, and I ended up walking around downtown, trying to cool off. I wanted to tell you last night, but you were asleep when I got here."

"You went walking downtown by *yourself*? At *night*?" Francie asked disbelievingly.

"No. . . . Well . . . for a while." Sydney put both hands to her aching head. "Then I rode the Amtrak down the coast to Solana Beach and back."

Francie stared, amazed. "Should I even ask?"

"The train station's right there. Tickets are cheap. I was crazed. . . ." Sydney shook her head. "The worst part is, Burke wanted to see me last night and I had to blow him off to meet my father. I think he's starting to get mad at me."

"I'm not surprised," Francie said again.

"Well, at least I don't have to worry about making any more time for my dad. After the fight we had, he was probably on the first plane to Brazil."

"They don't have a train?" Francie asked, raising one brow.

"Very funny. Trust me, Francie, he's gone."

"He wouldn't leave town without saying good-bye."

"Yes, he would."

"Are you sure?"

"Yes. . . . No." Sydney heaved a sigh. "I don't know."

Francie's features softened. "If he did, it's his loss."

"I guess. Listen, do you want to get some breakfast? I'll just pull on some sweats and—"

"I can't. I'm meeting Shauna and Carly for breakfast."

"Oh." Sydney's shoulders slumped. She could have really used a friend.

"I would have eaten with you," Francie said defensively. "But I didn't know you were going to be around."

Asking if they could all go to breakfast together was obviously out of the question. Sydney found herself getting angry all over again remembering the way Shauna and Carly had excluded her Tuesday night. "Maybe if your schedule wasn't so full of Shauna and Carly," she accused, "I wouldn't need an appointment just to—"

"Don't even go there. You have got to be kidding me!" Francie held up a warning hand. "If you weren't always so busy with your precious bank, I wouldn't *need* Shauna and Carly and we wouldn't be having this discussion."

"But—"

"Correction—we *aren't* having this discussion. You've already made me late."

With a toss of her head, Francie headed out the door, slamming it behind her.

"Great," Sydney said, flopping backward onto her mattress. "The perfect start to another perfect day."

* * *

"You're sure you're all right by yourself?" Rachel asked. "That copier can be pretty cranky."

"I'm an expert at cranky," Sydney said. "But if I get stuck, I'll call you."

"I'd better get back to the front desk, then. Jamia will be wondering what's happened to me by now."

"See you in a while," Sydney said, doing her best to make her voice bored. Rachel might get suspicious if she seemed too happy about making four copies each of three phone books' worth of engineering reports. But she was. Working by herself in the copy room would give her plenty of time to use her eraser mike to listen through the walls.

Too bad Owen isn't here today, she thought.

Not that she was likely to be allowed anywhere near him after the cake incident, but at least she was still allowed in the building. She could get a stack of copies going, then do a bit of snooping.

Maybe I'll run into Noah again.

The thought gave her a pang. She hadn't even talked to Noah since Monday, when he'd bailed her out of the upstairs library. She missed him, but she hadn't had time to track him down. At least she knew he understood when she couldn't be around. He was the only one who did.

He's probably here somewhere, she thought, removing a half-inch thickness of paper from one of the reports. Rachel had already programmed the copier to make four collated copies, so Sydney filled the automatic feeder, pressed Start, and stepped back, watching copies chug into trays. She waited until she was sure all was well, then turned her attention to more important things.

Pulling Graham's pen from her pocket, she pretended to jot a note while switching on the receiver already in her ear. Then she took out her eraser mike and wandered to the nearest wall, hoping to record something interesting.

At first all she heard was static. She pressed down on her ear, trying to tune her receiver to the signal the mike was sending. Faint sound came through in short, garbled bursts, as if she were spinning a radio dial in the desert. Giving up, she put the eraser back in her pocket—and suddenly she heard voices.

"It's almost finished," a man's deeply muffled voice said. "A few more days, and I'll be ready to make the swap. Are things in place on your end?"

"My client is ready with half." The second male voice was loud and clear. "Half on delivery; the other half when we verify the program works."

"That wasn't the agreement!"

Irritation made the first voice sharper, and Sydney gasped as she realized who it belonged to. Owen Vincent *was* in the building . . . and so was Robert Armstrong. She had picked up the signal from the edible bug.

Trembling with excitement, she hit the record button on her pen.

"We are fully prepared to meet your price," Armstrong said in a soothing tone. "But we need assurances."

"So do I," Vincent snapped. "Once you fire that puppy up, all hell's going to break loose here. I don't want to be around then, and if you're smart, neither do you. Pay in advance—or someone else will."

"Perhaps we can arrange a trial from outside the country?"

"And then you stiff me and I'm S.O.L. Not a chance. You want to hijack other people's missiles? Pay me first."

Sydney felt the air seep from her lungs. Wilson had guessed SST was up to something involving missile guidance, but if she understood what Vincent was driving at . . .

"What if they change the security codes on the satellites?" Armstrong asked. "What if we can't hack into the system to reroute the missiles we choose? What if—"

"Is that what you're paying me for? Or am I wrong?" Vincent's voice crackled with anger. "I think we're done here, Bob. I obviously have a few calls to make."

"No! No, all right. We'll pay. In advance. I'll have the money ready."

"Make sure you do. Because if your client tries to screw me, I might test the program myself."

* * *

"Brilliant!" Wilson crowed, removing his head-phones after hearing the playback a second time.

He and Sydney were sitting in his office, evaluating the conversation she'd recorded at SST. Sydney had been so excited that she'd rushed straight to him after her intern shift, despite the fact she was still dressed as Kristin Jarvis. Her makeup was intact, although her uncomfortable blond wig now lay on the seat of an extra chair.

"You've cracked it, Sydney," he said, beaming.

"And it's on tape," she added proudly. "That ought to help at trial."

Wilson's analysis had matched her own: Owen Vincent's software enabled its user to hack into the satellite guidance system of airborne missiles, potentially turning a country's own missiles against it or "stealing" them for use on completely different targets. The program was a terrorist's dream. Worse, the potential for international misunderstandings was huge. What would India do, for example, if one of Pakistan's "test" missiles landed on the Taj Mahal?

"It's going to be very helpful," he said. "But before we arrest anybody, we need to play this out—*and* we need that program. If Vincent hasn't actually finished it, and he hasn't actually sold anything . . ."

"Then we don't actually have a case," Sydney finished for him.

"Exactly. Not to mention the applications that

software could have for our military. I want it, Sydney. If anyone's going to use that program, it might as well be us."

"So what do we do next?"

"I'll call a meeting tomorrow morning. We'll get you and Noah in here together. Graham too . . . maybe a few other agents. Now that we know what Vincent's up to, we ought to be able to firm up a plan."

"Not tomorrow morning," Sydney begged. "I have a history quiz."

Wilson laughed. "And world peace hangs on that?"

"No, but my grade might. If you don't want to see me in summer school . . ."

"Come right after your quiz, then," he said, relenting. "I guess we can spare a couple more hours, since the program's not finished anyway."

"I'll be here. But speaking of quizzes, I'd better get going now. I have some studying to do."

"Knock 'em dead. See you tomorrow."

She was halfway out his door when he unexpectedly spoke again. "And Sydney? Fantastic work. You just keep getting better."

She flashed him a thrilled smile, ecstatic to have earned his praise, and all the way to the elevator she never felt the floor. She actually had to blink back tears as she stepped into the empty car.

Everything else in her life might be chaos, but Wilson knew how hard she was trying. He was the only person who understood how much she sacrificed every day—and how much she had accomplished.

If my dad was half the father Wilson is to me . . . , she thought, blinking harder.

But he wasn't, and he never would be.

The elevator doors opened on SD-6's subterranean garage. Sydney stepped out and headed for her rental car, her mind already turning to all the things she still had to do that day: Drive back to the gym, change into her regular clothes, ditch the makeup and—

"Wig!" she groaned, smacking herself in the forehead.

For a moment she considered leaving it in Wilson's office and picking it up the next morning. But it didn't seem smart to leave the building wearing only half a disguise, and it could be downright dangerous to show up at school that way. If someone she knew recognized her . . .

"Good work, Supersleuth," she muttered, turning around and stepping back into the elevator.

Wilson was still in his office when she went down the hall. His door was closed, but she could see him hunched over his computer through an interior window. She stood indecisively, watching him work, wondering if she should knock or just walk in. She hated that she even had to bother him—especially after just leaving on such a high note.

Her boss was totally absorbed in whatever he was doing. His fingers picked over the keyboard so slowly he couldn't be typing English; he had to be working in code. His obvious concentration made interrupting him even less appealing, but waiting wasn't going to make it any better. Taking a deep breath, Sydney eased his office door open, hoping to disturb him as little as possible.

She had done it so quietly he didn't notice. She could see his monitor now, slowly filling up with a code she hadn't yet learned. Feeling incredibly awkward, wishing she'd knocked after all, Sydney cleared her throat.

"Sydney!" Wilson pushed back from the computer so fast he nearly upset his chair. Regaining his balance, he reached over and hit a key, blanking out his screen. "How long have you been there?"

"I'm sorry. I just . . ." She walked over and grabbed her wig, holding it up for him to see. "I should have knocked."

"Well, yes. But that's all right. I wasn't doing anything important."

Sydney's breath caught in her chest. Wilson was a total pro; nothing ever showed on his face. But he was nervous now. And he was lying. She had never seen him so flustered.

"Sorry," she repeated, backing out of his office and closing the door.

Her second trip to the elevator wasn't nearly as joyous as her first.

The fact that Wilson was sending code on his computer should have been a nonevent. He was a spy. That was what spies did. But the way he'd reacted when he saw her . . .

There were levels of security clearance at SD-6, and his was well above hers. Whatever Wilson was working on had most likely exceeded her clearance.

But still . . .

So I saw a few lines of code, she thought. *Obviously I have no idea what it meant, or who he was sending it to.*

The elevator came and Sydney stepped into the car, her wig dangling forgotten from one hand.

But I'd like to. And what I'd really like to know is, why did Wilson look so guilty?

7

"SO HOW DID YOU do?" Burke asked Sydney. "Let me guess—you nailed it."

They had just emerged from the dim American history lecture hall into the bright sunshine outside, but Sydney's move to shade her eyes had more to do with not wanting to meet his gaze.

"I bombed," she said, her throat tight with disappointment. "I tried to study last night, but I have so much on my mind . . . When I woke up this morning I'd forgotten everything."

"You bombed," Burke teased. "What does that

mean in Sydney-speak? You got a B instead of an A?"

"I *failed*, Burke," she said sharply, dropping her shading hand to look him in the face. "What part of *bombed* don't you understand?"

"It couldn't be as bad as—"

"It is! And I don't want to talk about it anymore."

"Okay." He looked away from her, his eyes full of hurt confusion.

"I mean, I don't want to talk about how *I* did," she amended quickly. "How about you?"

Burke shrugged, from which she deduced he'd found it easy. "It's just a quiz. This grade hardly matters."

Maybe not to you, Sydney thought.

If Burke really understood her, he'd know how much she hated to fail at anything. With all the things she was juggling, it was unavoidable that something would fall through the cracks now and then, but that didn't mean she let herself slide. She couldn't—she wasn't wired that way.

"Besides," Burke added, trying to cheer her up. "If you ace the final, you'll still get an A in the class."

"Right." Never mind that all the information

she'd just forgotten would be on the final too. Burke didn't get it, and for once she didn't suffer from the urge to explain it to him. There were so many things about her he could never understand; if they were going to be together, she'd have to get used to that. "I guess I'll see you later."

"This weekend?" he asked hopefully.

"It's possible." Although it didn't seem very likely. SpaceSoft was closed on weekends, but there was no way of knowing what else Wilson had planned for her. Not to mention that there was only a week left to study before finals started . . . "I'll call you."

"Really?"

She tried to meet his eyes, then looked away in defeat. "I don't know," she admitted.

"Two more weeks," he reminded her. "Then finals are over, and you're going to be all caught up. We have an entire summer in front of us."

She shrugged noncommittally, her head bobbing in a motion that wasn't quite a nod. How could she tell him she couldn't make summer promises either?

"Right?" he persisted.

"I guess. But now I really have to go."

"Me too. If I sprint all the way across campus, I *might* still get to chem on time."

He dropped a kiss on her forehead, then turned and started running, his long hair and loose cotton shirt flapping out behind him. His leather sandals slapped the sidewalk. His woven book bag bounced and swung to his rhythm. Sydney watched him disappear, a smile flitting over her lips.

He looks so free, she thought.

And I'm so . . . not.

Checking her watch, she felt her pulse thud into high gear. She'd promised Wilson she'd meet him at SD-6 right after her quiz. He'd be waiting for her now.

And with any luck, so would Noah.

* * *

"Let's go in there and take it," Noah proposed. "Give me five men in body armor and those rent-a-guards at SST won't even know what hit them."

"Commando style," Graham said, looking impressed.

"You're not going in there shooting," Sydney objected, thinking of all the innocent people who'd get hurt.

"I won't have to," Noah replied with a wink. "We'll come in the front door and take you hostage. Say we're going to kill you if they don't cooperate."

"Whatever happened to serving a warrant?" she asked, hoping he was joking.

"I don't like it," Agent Westin said. "Sydney's new there, and not in the least important. Who's to say they won't call your bluff and sacrifice her?"

"Nobody's sacrificing anyone," Wilson said impatiently. He lurched to his feet, looming over the head of the conference room's long polished table. "I said I wanted a *plan*. And so far I haven't heard one."

In addition to Sydney, Noah, and Graham, Wilson had invited two senior agents to the tactical meeting, neither of whom Sydney had met before. Agent Westin was tall, blond, and in possession of very long legs beneath a short black skirt; she crossed and uncrossed them repeatedly, as if to make sure everyone noticed. Agent Barret was older, shorter, and conservatively dressed. He hadn't said a thing since the introductions, but his eyes flicked from speaker to speaker with total concentration.

"Barret!" Wilson barked. "Ideas?"

Agent Barret looked from Wilson to Noah then back again. "Force is always an option, but quieter is better."

"Exactly," said Wilson. "Besides, the software's

not even done yet. I want a finished product, not a bunch of useless code."

"Excuse me, sir," Graham piped in, "but if I could see what Vincent's already done, I could probably finish it. I mean, I'm not bragging, but—"

"You were saying, Barret?" Wilson interrupted.

"We could offer to buy the software. Outbid whoever Armstrong's client is."

"Now that's a plan," Wilson said approvingly. "Work on that. See if you can set us up as buyers."

Barret nodded and, to Sydney's surprise, left the room.

He doesn't fool around, she thought. *Maybe that's why Wilson invited him.*

The reason for Agent Westin's presence was still a mystery.

Could be those legs.

Not that Wilson was paying them any obvious attention. In fact, he seemed distracted, pacing, then sitting, then pacing again. He had barely acknowledged Sydney when she'd come in. That hadn't seemed weird at the time, since the meeting was already in progress, but the way he'd been avoiding her eyes ever since was starting to get obvious. The more he didn't look at her, the more she stared at him, tracking him around the room.

As if feeling her gaze, he stopped abruptly and turned to face her.

"Sydney."

"What?" she asked, startled.

"You're not saying much."

"I didn't know you wanted me to."

"You must have some ideas." Wilson's hand went to his tie, tugging at the knot as if he found it too tight.

"Sydney and I could steal it," Noah jumped in. "With all the people who work in that building, theft would involve more finesse, but it could be done."

"That's better," said Wilson. "I'll keep it in mind."

He glanced Sydney's way again, then paced to the other side of the room. His hand returned to his tie.

Is he nervous? Sydney couldn't remember ever seeing him play with his tie before—and it wasn't as if he wasn't used to wearing one. *Why would he be nervous?*

Maybe it had something to do with Agent Westin, although Sydney couldn't imagine what; Wilson was the one who'd invited her in the first place. She turned her attention to Noah, to see if he'd noticed anything unusual, but he met her questioning look with a confused shrug.

I'm imagining it, she thought.

"Here's what we're going to do," Wilson announced, planting both hands on the tabletop and leaning forward to address them all. "Westin, you work with Barret. If he can set up a buy, you'll pose as our buyer. Start putting together a cover and requisition some cash."

Agent Westin nodded, clearly pleased with that assignment.

"Graham, give Noah an earpiece for the bug in Armstrong's gut. If he comes back for a second discussion, I want to make double sure we hear it."

"Will do!" Graham said.

"Noah, as soon as you get that gear, head straight back to SST. Do not leave that building unless and until Owen Vincent does. Keep him under constant surveillance."

Noah nodded. Sydney could tell he was still chafing to do something more aggressive, but Wilson was calling the shots.

"Sydney," Wilson said finally. "Work your regular intern shift today. Keep your ears open and your head down. Now that we know what's going on, I don't want you taking any risks."

"I won't."

"That's everything, then," he said. "Any questions?"

His tone suggested it might be better if there weren't.

"All right. Get going." Wilson pushed his weight off the table, back onto his feet. On the high-polished wood where his hands had been, two sweaty palm prints remained, every finger distinct.

Sydney's brows jumped; the room wasn't remotely hot. In almost the same instant, a folder hit the table, covering the prints. Sydney looked up to find Wilson's eyes trained on the doorway, his jaw set and tense.

"I have some paperwork," he said. "I'll just finish it here."

Noah, Graham, and Westin rose to leave, and Sydney had no choice but to follow.

Out in the hallway, she pulled Noah off to one side.

"When am I going to see you again?" she whispered.

He smiled, pleased. "This afternoon, if you want to hang out in my janitor's closet." He shoved his hands into the front pockets of his SST coveralls, pushing out the baggy legs until they looked ridiculous. "Come on, baby. You *know* you want to," he added, waggling his eyebrows.

"I miss you," she admitted. "But maybe not enough for those pants."

"Snob."

"Slacker."

He let go of his coveralls, his face growing serious. "I've missed you too," he said. "How was dinner with your father?"

"Don't ask! I mean, I'd tell you, but not here. I was hoping maybe you and I could . . ."

Could what? She didn't even know.

"I just miss you," she repeated. "And I'm having a bad week."

She wished she could snuggle into his arms for comfort, but there was no chance of that at SD-6. At best, they could pretend to discuss their joint mission a minute longer, and then they'd have to break it up.

To her amazement, however, Noah reached forward and touched her hand. "This gig can't last much longer, and then we'll have some time. Next weekend we'll do something fun, I promise. I mean . . . you know, assuming we're both in town."

"Right," she agreed, choking up. Her fingers brushed against his, feeling the warmth of his skin, before she reluctantly let him go. "See you soon."

Noah walked off down the hall to get his new earpiece and Sydney watched him go, temporarily lost.

Now what? she wondered.

Her orders were to go play intern at SST, her heart yearned to follow Noah, and her overriding inclination was to drop back in on Wilson and ask him what he was up to.

Not that he'd answer me.

If something big was going on, she was almost certainly too low on the SD-6 totem pole to be let in on the secret. The realization annoyed her. The CIA didn't mind asking her to risk her life, but they still didn't trust her. It didn't seem right, somehow.

Even so, Wilson wouldn't have to tell me if I figured it out myself. The thought hit Sydney out of nowhere, rocking her with its implications.

Wilson had a secret. And he had recruited and trained her specifically to bring secrets to light.

She headed for the elevator, her mind made up.

I have to intern this afternoon and study tomorrow morning. But after that there's nothing to stop me from doing a little freelance surveillance.

On Wilson.

* * *

Sydney wasn't sorry to find her dorm room dark when she got home. She'd already had a long stressful day, and the last thing she needed was more drama with Francie. Walking to her built-in desk, she switched on the little lamp and shrugged her backpack off her tired shoulders.

A handwritten note from Francie rested in the center of her blotter, weighed down by a thick chocolate bar:

> *Hi, Syd!*
> *Shauna's selling candy bars to raise money for crew. I bought this one for you. If you want to meet us, we're at the Lion's Den. Remember that band you missed when the bank sent you to San Diego? They're playing again tonight. No cover! See you there?*
> *Francie*

Sydney read the note twice, not sure how to feel. Despite the unappetizing fact that Shauna had been involved, the chocolate was clearly intended as a peace offering. Plus, she had finally been invited to hang out with Francie's new friends—which was good. Except that she couldn't go—which was bad. Would ignoring Francie's invitation make things worse between them?

Maybe I can catch Francie on her cell phone and explain how I failed that quiz, Sydney thought. *That would be better than just not showing up.*

So long as she put the emphasis on finals and avoided mentioning work, Francie would probably take it pretty well. Especially since she was already having fun with her other friends.

Sydney was putting the note back down when she noticed the tiny arrow pointing to the edge of the paper. A postscript had been added to the back:

P.S. Your dad left a message on the answering machine. I saved it for you.

"What now?" Sydney groaned. "So much for a drama-free evening."

Dragging her feet across the shabby carpet, Sydney made her way to the answering machine, hesitating with one finger just over the button.

Should I push it? Or do myself a favor and hit Erase?

Bracing herself for the worst, Sydney pressed the button.

"Sydney . . . this is your father," said an uncharacteristically tentative voice. "I think I stepped in it the other night. I wanted to say I'm sorry."

She gasped with genuine amazement.

"I wasn't trying to tell you what to do," he continued. "Which is to say I was, but I thought you might *enjoy* the London program. If you'd rather work, I'll understand. I guess you're old enough to start making your own decisions."

Her knees buckled. Her rear end hit her mattress.

"I assume you have Saturdays off. Meet me at the Santa Monica Pier tomorrow, say ten o'clock? We'll spend the day together."

Sydney sat in silent shock long after the message had ended. Her father was still in town after all. Even more astonishing, *he'd* apologized to *her*. And if a father-daughter day didn't top her list of fun activities, it suddenly seemed more important than anything else she had to do.

He's making an effort. So will I.

If they were ever going to have a normal relationship, they had to start somewhere.

8

SYDNEY DROVE HER MUSTANG into the huge beachside lot at the Santa Monica Pier on Saturday morning, breathing a sigh of relief when she saw empty parking spaces. It was only ten o'clock, but the pier's popular amusement park had already been open for an hour, and the way the sun was shining was sure to make people think of the beach. Parking in the nearest space, Sydney grabbed a small gift-wrapped package from her passenger seat, stuffed it into a straw tote, and slung the bag over one shoulder. Then she headed toward the pier, as tired as if she'd already put in a full day.

In a way, she had. Up at dawn to study for three hours, she'd snuck out of her dorm room and showered without waking Francie, then hurried to an off-campus deli for a bagel she'd eaten standing up. From there it had been another short walk to a book and stationery shop, where she'd selected a gift and had it wrapped, practically sprinting from there back to the school parking lot where she kept her Mustang. Now, crossing the wide open area between her parking space and the pier, she wished she'd thought to wear a windbreaker along with her tank top and shorts. The sun was warm, but the salty breeze off the ocean was cool and wild, blowing stray strands of hair across her eyes and mouth.

It'll be warmer among the buildings, Sydney reassured herself. Farther out, over the ocean, the pier narrowed to the standard dimension. But closer in, over the beach and shallows, the structure was seven times wider, an enormous, gritty platform supporting a fun zone, roller coaster, and vintage carousel inside a historic building.

And then she saw her father and forgot everything else.

Jack Bristow was leaning against a railing, looking out to sea. The wind blew his hair straight back off his face and brought unusual color to his cheeks. His posture was relaxed, his expression miles away. But most surprising of all, he had shed his usual dark suit in favor of linen slacks and a light blue polo shirt. Sydney blinked hard at the sight of him. She'd seen her father wear normal clothes before, but it had been so long that she'd forgotten how different he looked.

"Dad, hi!" she called, stepping onto the weathered boards.

Jack's head snapped to attention. His body stiffened, and by the time she'd reached the railing, his face had transformed itself into his usual mask. Sydney's spirits sank. For just a moment, before he'd seen her, she had almost believed that this time would be different.

"Hi, Dad," she repeated awkwardly. "I, uh . . . hi. Nice day."

Jack nodded, then looked back out to sea. "I was just thinking the people on those sailboats must be having fun."

"The wind's a little fluky for sailing," Sydney replied without thinking. "Too many gusts. Plus it's probably clocked forty-five degrees just since I got here."

Jack's face registered mild surprise. His eyes held hers, awaiting an explanation.

Oops, Sydney thought, too late.

As far as her father knew, her experience with

boats was limited to paddling canoes at summer camp. She could hardly tell him her CIA recruiter was making sure she got trained at the helm of every major class of vessel.

She gave him a sheepish smile. "Some of the kids in my dorm are windsurfers. Wind is all they talk about. Honestly, it gets kind of boring, but if you hang around them long enough, you can't help picking it up. We'll be eating lunch outside our building and a piece of trash will blow by and they'll be, like, 'Dude! Totally ridable!'"

"Um, yes," said her father, shaking his head. "Shall we?"

He gestured down the pier, where people milled about in brightly colored summer clothes and the sounds of a clacking roller coaster and the accompanying screams drifted back over the surf. Sydney followed as he led the way.

"So," she said to his back. "Can you believe it's June tomorrow? The year went by so fast."

He walked a few more paces, then abruptly stopped and turned around. They had reached the beginning of the fun zone.

"What do you want to do first?" he asked, putting on a strangely enthusiastic expression. "One of the rides? Maybe play the arcade?"

"Well—I—I—" she stammered, at a loss.

He was doing it again. He was treating her like she was eight years old. Having Daddy take her places like Olvera Street and the pier was something she'd dreamed about then, but now the exotic sights and happy normal people just seemed like a way to distract her from the things that really mattered.

"We *could* walk around and talk," she suggested.

"Talk?" he said warily. "About what?"

"I don't know. When are you going back to South America?"

"Soon."

"I don't even know where you're staying over there. Tell me the coolest thing you've seen."

"I'm constantly moving," he said vaguely. "And it sounds more exciting than it is. Mostly I see the insides of airplanes and hotels."

"But you must—"

"I'll bet I can knock down those cans!" he said, pointing to a nearby carnival game. A dollar bought three attempts for anyone foolish enough to believe they could upend lead-weighted jugs with a baseball.

"Those games are all fixed."

"Everything's fixed. But there's always a trick—you just have to know what it is."

She followed grudgingly as he plowed ahead, slapping a dollar down on the worn wooden railing.

"I'll have a go," he told the attendant.

The bored-looking man took his money and passed across three baseballs.

"It's all about balance," Jack told Sydney, winding up his arm. "Striking in just the right spot is key."

He unleashed his first baseball with astonishing force. In the split second before it slammed into the milk jugs and ricocheted harmlessly into a corner, Sydney realized she'd never seen him throw one before.

"Balance," she echoed ironically, her eyes on the undisturbed jugs. "I can see what a difference it makes."

"Wait," he told her, holding up his second ball.

She watched him throw that one, as well as his third and three more, before he finally admitted defeat and allowed her to coax him to the pier-edge railing.

"You almost had it a couple of times," she said consolingly. "They definitely wobbled."

Jack rubbed his pitching shoulder. "My aim was off. I used to be able to do that."

"You probably still could, if you practiced."

"You think so?" He brightened, then sighed and

shook his head. "I don't have much time for baseball, and I can't say I see that changing. Everything passes. Those days are over."

His expression became melancholy. His gaze sought the sailboats again.

"I brought you something," Sydney said, feeling a sudden need to cheer him up. Reaching into her tote bag, she extracted the slim gift-wrapped package. "It's actually a Father's Day present, but you probably won't be here then. . . ."

She waited for him to contradict her. He didn't.

"Open it," she urged, thrusting it toward him.

Jack took the package reluctantly, stripping off its paper and bow. He flipped the hinged box open and froze, his expression unreadable.

"It's real silver," Sydney said nervously, not sure whether he liked the fountain pen she'd chosen.

"It's too expensive."

"Not if you like it. I mean, the bank pays me pretty well."

He looked at her at last. "All right, then. If the *bank's* paying for it . . ." He slipped the pen into his slacks pocket. "Thank you."

"You're welcome," she replied, feeling formal and awkward and awful again. Couldn't he at least smile? "It reminded me of you."

"Oh?"

"Of when I was little. You had that favorite pen, remember? Mom used to always tease you about using it on the Sunday crossword puzzle."

A door slammed shut behind his eyes. "I don't do crosswords anymore."

"No. But . . . do you remember?" she asked hopefully.

They never talked about her mother; Laura Bristow's short life and violent death were a dangerously off-limits topic. But just this once, Sydney wanted to talk about it anyway. That crushing loss—and all the pain that had followed—was the one thing she and her dad had in common.

"Not at the moment," Jack said.

"You must," she insisted. "Every Sunday you'd get the paper and I'd read the comics and Mom—"

"Ice cream!" Jack called, hailing a passing cart. "What would you like, Sydney?"

"It's too early for ice cream," she said, resenting the interruption.

Her father didn't take the hint. "Give me two of those," he told the vendor, pointing to a picture on the side of the cooler.

Money changed hands, and the next thing Sydney knew, her father was forcing an enormous ice cream sandwich on her.

"I can't eat all that," she protested, even though

the bagel she'd had for breakfast was a distant memory.

"Then just eat what you want. This should be a fun day. No rules. And no heavy discussions."

That sounds like a rule to me, she thought sullenly, biting into her ice cream.

Around her the pier was filling up, alive with families and teens and tourists in unfortunate shorts. Everyone scurried this way and that, holding hands, pointing, laughing. Sydney stood silently beside her father, the two of them just killing time.

I should have stayed home and slept in.

No matter how hard she tried, she would never connect with her father. Even the effort was exhausting.

A horrified shriek reached Sydney above the other noises. She turned her head to see a pink balloon float up and sideways on the breeze, a distraught toddler crying beneath it. In almost the same instant, the child was scooped up by a man who carried her back to the balloon seller, overcoming her tears with a new purple one, tying its ribbon tightly to her wrist, making everything all right. . . .

Sydney glanced from the little girl to Jack, hoping for some reaction. Her father was still eating ice cream and staring across the waves, apparently fascinated now by the buildings crowding the shore.

It's hopeless, she thought, giving up. *He and I aren't a family; we're just a couple of tourists.*

* * *

Sydney eased into a more comfortable position in the driver's seat of her Mustang, wondering if she'd lost her mind.

This is nuts; he could stay in there for hours. Not to mention that I'm dead if he sees me sitting out here. I'll never explain this one!

She wished she'd at least brought one of her textbooks, to make better use of her time. History would have been the smart move, or that poetry anthology she needed to read for her literature class.

One more hour, she decided. *If Wilson doesn't come out in an hour, I'll forget about this and go back to the dorm.*

Her father thought she was already there. She had stuck with him long enough to eat lunch on the pier, then begged off for the rest of the day, saying she had to study. She had even intended to do that. But a different impulse had possessed her when she'd seen the pier in her rearview mirror. Or repossessed her, actually, since the idea of spying on

Wilson had first occurred to her the day before. Even so, she could barely believe she was doing it. Wilson's behavior wasn't even that strange so much as just out of character for a guy who was usually so—

Uh-oh, she thought, sliding low in her seat. *Here we go.*

Her boss's black SUV was leaving the parking garage. From where she'd parked on the main street, Sydney could just see it nosing out. She waited until Wilson had nearly disappeared into traffic, then pulled out to follow him.

I should have switched to my rental car, she realized, too late. *Wilson's never seen that one.*

Although now that she thought about it, she couldn't remember him ever seeing her Mustang, either. The main thing was just to stay back far enough to keep him from noticing her.

It wasn't easy. Wilson wove through the streets of downtown L.A. at high speed, making last-second turns and unsignaled lane changes like a man who was used to avoiding a tail. He'd been doing it for so long it had become automatic to him. Sydney had to struggle to keep him in view.

She had followed him out of the city center and into a hilly suburban neighborhood when all of a sudden she made a turn and felt her stomach drop.

There was no other car in sight. She'd lost him.

He must have turned down a side street, she thought, hitting her brakes in the middle of the quiet residential road. Her heart pounded with uncertainty. Should she go forward or circle back? She couldn't stay where she was; curtains were beginning to twitch as residents peeked out their windows, suspicious of the unknown car stopped in their street.

Stepping on the gas, Sydney continued forward. She had just decided to make a U-turn at the next intersection when a flash of movement caught her eye: At a sprawling house set back from the left-hand side of the road, a black SUV was rolling to a stop at the end of a long driveway.

There's his car!

She accelerated past the house, praying Wilson didn't look behind him. Two blocks farther down she turned left, driving about half a mile before she happened upon a horse and hiking trailhead with several cars parked haphazardly in the packed dirt around it. Ditching her Mustang there, she began jogging back to where she'd last seen the SUV.

Was that his house, or is he visiting someone? she wondered as she ran, using the neighborhood's tall hedges and other landscaping for cover. SD-6 didn't print a directory of employee names, let alone addresses and phone numbers, so Sydney had no idea where Wilson lived. The house could belong to anyone.

Maybe he's meeting a contact. Or a girlfriend!

The thought of no-nonsense Wilson carrying on a clandestine love affair almost made her laugh out loud. She swallowed her giggles as she rounded the final corner and took up a position behind a huge pine tree. She leaned against its trunk, lifting a foot and pretending to stretch her quads for anyone who might be watching, but her gaze was fixed on the mouth of the driveway Wilson had driven down.

Should she wait for him to come out? Should she try to get closer and see what he was doing inside? Every bit of common sense told her to turn around and trot home, but common sense wasn't running the show anymore. Something deeper, some gut instinct, made her stick with Wilson.

She'd been stalling at the tree ten minutes and was running out of muscles to stretch when Wilson suddenly appeared on foot, headed directly toward her. He was wearing a blue nylon track suit, which looked amazingly odd on a man of his large frame. Or perhaps his spanking white Adidas were what kept the outfit from being convincing. But the most telling detail of all, the thing that nearly stopped her heart, was the tightly folded newspaper he held tucked beneath one arm. Runners didn't carry newspapers. If she hadn't learned anything else on the track team, she felt confident of that.

Wilson was on some sort of mission. And he was about to bust her big-time.

9

STAY CALM, STAY CALM, stay calm, Sydney told herself, totally freaking out.

She plastered her body against the tree trunk, ignoring the sticky sap that ruined her tank top and marked her bare arms. The insanity of her actions was completely apparent to her now, but unfortunately, her escape route was not. She could hear Wilson striding toward her down the sidewalk, nearer every second. Meanwhile, she was quaking behind a pine tree without a plan, without a disguise, without even a good excuse.

At least it's a big tree. Plus, so far as she could

tell, no one was watching her. She took a baby step to the left, timing her move by the sound of Wilson's approaching footsteps.

She still couldn't see him. She prayed that meant he couldn't see her.

Another baby step. Another.

He was almost to the tree. Another step.

Sydney held her breath. . . .

She could hear his footfalls on the sidewalk directly across the trunk from her, maybe six feet away. Then he was past.

Another step, moving more quickly now. She caught a split-second glimpse of his back as she slid around the tree.

She was safe.

That was too close! she thought, slumping against the trunk. *I never want to do that again.*

But a moment later she was back on the hunt, tracking Wilson down the sidewalk.

My car's in this direction anyway, she rationalized.

She followed at a distance, letting Wilson get a good lead before dashing to the next bit of cover. At the corner, he turned right.

That's a gift. Take it, said a little voice in her head. All she had to do was let him get out of sight, then run left to her car and disappear. Instead, she followed him to the right, ignoring the alarms going off in her brain.

Within a couple of curvy blocks, the houses on the other side of the road gave way to a long, brushy hill. Sydney imagined the horse trail she'd noticed before winding along the hill's low crest, but eucalyptus trees and thick vegetation made it impossible to see if that was the case. She considered dashing to that side of the road, where the natural landscape offered more cover, but before she could make up her mind, Wilson beat her to it. Sydney stepped into hiding behind a manicured yellow hibiscus, waiting to see where he'd go.

About a hundred yards ahead, the brushy hill dipped down to a saddle containing a crossroad. Wilson turned left at the corner, skirting the end of the hill. Sydney let him get out of sight, then ran across the street, pushing forcefully through the dense vegetation on her way straight up the hill.

The ground wasn't steep, but progress was more difficult than she'd expected. Low-lying shoots and tendrils caught her feet. A thorny bougainvillea gouged scratches in her bare legs. Her shorts snagged on a tree branch, which ripped a hole in their fabric, while dust and dirt darkened the sap on her shirt and arms.

It's got to be right up here, she thought, fighting

her way between two stubborn bushes near the crest. *If I'm right about that trail, it ought to be . . .*

Bingo.

Directly ahead of her, the vegetation ended abruptly, pounded into a wide dirt path by generations of hooves and sneakers. The trail was deserted, and Sydney charged onto it eagerly, sprinting in the direction Wilson had headed.

Her plan was to stay above him, tracking him on the street from her shelter in the trees. But she hadn't gone very far when the trail took an abrupt left turn, and Sydney didn't have the heart to battle forward through more bushes.

I'll just stay with this and see where I come out.

In such a suburban area, there was no chance of ending up lost in the woods. The path was sure to come out near a street, hopefully the same one Wilson had taken. She kept to the trail and a minute later saw a break in the trees up ahead. A few steps farther along, grass appeared through the opening. The trail was about to end in a park.

Stepping quickly off the path, Sydney crept forward through cover of trees and bushes to a hidden viewing place near the edge of the grass. She could see Wilson's road in the distance, bordering the park's far edge, but he wasn't there. Perhaps she had gotten ahead of him with her shortcut. If she waited where she was, she might still see him walk past. Or perhaps . . .

Perhaps Wilson was sitting on a bench in the center of the park, calmly reading his newspaper.

Too weird! she thought, backing deeper into the bushes. *What is he doing?*

The idea of her energetic and impatient handler killing time on a park bench was too surreal to accept. But there he was, surrounded by joggers, Frisbee players, and mothers with tots, his bright blue running suit unmistakable.

He can't be meeting a contact in the park, she thought disbelievingly. *That's like a spy cliché!*

Not only that, but she'd been certain the newspaper he carried concealed some sort of intel. The possibility that he might actually read it had never occurred to her.

He looks *like he's reading it,* she thought, still suspicious. *Maybe he's just turning pages.*

One of the joggers who had been warming up nearby dropped to the grass in front of Wilson's bench and began stretching his hamstrings.

If he's here to meet someone, that ought to shake him up, Sydney thought, trying to gauge Wilson's reaction. Her handler remained absorbed in his paper, holding it close to his face for better reading. She could just see his eyes over the top of the page, and they weren't showing the least sign of panic.

The runner stretched over one long leg, grabbing his foot and pulling his face down to his knee. As he did, Sydney thought she saw his lips move.

Unless he's here to meet that runner!

Was it possible? She couldn't see Wilson's mouth to tell if he was speaking.

Besides, even if that jogger said something, it doesn't mean he's a contact.

But everything seemed wrong to her now. All of her senses were on full alert. She edged a little closer, creeping cautiously through the bushes. If she got a better angle, maybe she could read the jogger's lips. . . .

And that was when Sydney noticed the third suspicious person in the park. Fifty feet behind Wilson, a homeless man dressed in filthy fatigues lurked at the edge of a small bathroom building. He was wearing dark glasses in the space between his stocking cap and unkempt beard, but Sydney could have sworn he was staring right at her. A thrill of fear shot down her spine. His gaze was so direct, so intense. . . . Could he see her?

Instinctively, she ducked.

When she peeked up again, the man had gone. Disappeared.

He's only stepped behind the building, she reassured herself. *He couldn't possibly have seen me.*

Nothing else had changed. Wilson was still reading, the jogger was still stretching. . . .

But Sydney's confidence was shot.

Had that shabby man been spying on *her*? Did he suspect who she was, or what she was doing? Because if he planned to discuss it with Wilson, she was going to be in some serious trouble.

Pushing frantically back through the brush to the trail, Sydney sprinted toward where she'd parked her car, running for all she was worth. She wasn't disguised. She wasn't armed. She wasn't even sure she was sane.

All I know is this is over. I've had enough free-lancing!

To: k.estrada@creditdauphine.com

From: jack.bristow@credit-dauphine.com

Subject: Delayed

Situation worse than anticipated.
Will be out a few more days.

10

"WILL YOU LOOK AT that weather?" Francie said happily, pouring syrup over her pancakes until it made amber pools on her plate. "Here comes summer!"

Light spilled through the floor-to-ceiling windows of the commons that Sunday morning, illuminating the tables and infusing the crowded dining room with an unusually laid-back atmosphere.

"Two more weeks," Sydney said, trying not to stress about everything she still had to do during that time. "Are you going to save some of that syrup for me?"

"Maybe." Francie held the little glass pitcher aloft. "Do you think you deserve it?"

"I'm doing this for your own good," Sydney said, making a grab. Her hand closed around the silver handle. "Aha!" she cried triumphantly, waving the pitcher over her head. Then, noticing the attention she was attracting from nearby tables, she quickly lowered it and started pouring.

"You're cracking up, Syd," Francie told her, smiling.

Sydney smiled back. "You mean I'm a crack-up."

"Believe what you want."

"Come on, you know you love me."

At least it was starting to seem that way again. Francie had been home when Sydney got back from the park the day before, full of sympathy upon hearing Sydney's impromptu tale of running out of gas and cutting through some unexpectedly deadly bushes on her walk to the nearest station. They had studied together for hours, capping off the evening with a well-deserved pizza and video. But the best part of all had been waking up in the morning and finding Francie waiting to go to breakfast with her, just like old times. Sydney didn't know where Shauna and Carly were, and she didn't care. She just hoped they stayed away.

"After this, maybe we can go to the library for a

couple of hours, then hit the beach," Francie said. "A person can't study *all* day."

"I can, and I'm going to."

Francie pulled a face, making Sydney reconsider. This was the first real attention her friend had paid her all week; she didn't want to blow it.

"But there's no good reason I can't study at the beach," she added.

Francie smiled broadly. "I'll bet the water's warm."

"And the sand is probably *hot,* so don't forget your flip-flops."

"One time!" Francie protested. "One time and you never let a girl—"

Sydney's pager went off, interrupting them with a series of beeps.

"Uh-oh," Francie said sarcastically. "The bank found out you were trying to get a life."

"They're psychic that way," Sydney said, trying not to assume the worst. Wilson *might* give her the day off, or at least let her come in later. . . .

But to her surprise, her pager read HICKS followed by three *X*s—Noah's code for urgent business.

"I have to go," she blurted out.

"I'm so shocked."

"I'm sorry, Francie, but this is important."

"Don't worry about it," Francie said coldly. "I'm pretty clear on what's important to you."

Sydney winced as the barb sank in. "I didn't mean you aren't important. It's just—"

"I don't want to hear it," Francie said, cutting her off. She stood and picked up her tray, looking for someplace new to sit.

"Maybe I can still get back in time to—"

"Don't bother," said Francie, walking away. She headed toward a packed table and wasn't halfway there before its occupants started calling her name and waving her over. Sydney scanned their faces, trying to recognize someone.

It didn't help her mood to realize she didn't know a single person there.

* * *

"Finally!" Noah exclaimed, motioning Sydney into the back of a janitor's van and closing the double doors behind her. "What took you so long?"

"Hello to you too," she said irritably. "This had better be important."

Following his telephone instructions, she had driven her rental car to meet him in a carpool lot a couple of miles from the SST building, but he hadn't said anything about holding a conference in the windowless back of a van. The vehicle was stuffy, cramped, and full of smells she didn't want to analyze too closely. Noah seemed oblivious to it all.

"It's done!" he told her, his brown eyes glittering with excitement. "Vincent just finished it."

"The missile program?" she asked, forgetting everything else. "How do you know?"

"I've been up with the guy for two nights, watching him through my feed in the janitor's closet. That little run-in with Armstrong must have been mighty motivational, because he hasn't slept since Friday." Noah pointed to a thermos lying on the floorboards. "Three cheers for coffee."

"But how do you know it's finished?" she persisted. "Maybe he just had to go to bed."

"I don't think so." Noah took her wrists, squeezing too hard. "He's been working alone in a classified computer lab, and about an hour ago he got up and started jumping around, dancing, acting like a complete moron. Before he left he locked a portable hard drive in the safe. That's it, Sydney. I'm telling you."

He peered deeply into her eyes, making her wonder if the glint in his was only excitement. Their glassiness suggested that more than caffeine might be keeping him awake.

"So . . . good," she said at last. "But I'm still not sure why I'm here."

"Because I'm going to steal it," he said. "And the way that lab's set up, I need a lookout."

Sydney shook his hands off her wrists. "Are you crazy? What about Barret and Westin, and setting up a buy?"

"Listen to me, Syd. That program is done, and for all we know it could be gone in another hour. We need to take it right now."

"We can't make that call on our own." That he would even suggest such a thing made her more concerned than ever that his judgment was impaired. "What would Wilson say?"

"He'll say 'Congratulations' and 'Thank you very much,'" Noah replied, reaching behind him. His hand came back with a pair of wadded blue coveralls, which he thrust at Sydney's midsection. "Here, put these on."

"I'm not doing this," she said, crossing her arms stubbornly.

Noah looked stunned for a moment. Then his eyes went narrow. "Oh, you're doing it. And you know why? Because I outrank you, that's why. Now put on that suit and hurry up."

Sydney faced him down. She'd seen his Jekyll-and-Hyde act before, and this time she wouldn't be intimidated. If she wanted to check with Wilson first, that was exactly what she'd do.

The problem was, she wasn't sure she wanted to. What if he knew about her spying on him the day before? Maybe he was just waiting for a chance to let her have it.

No, he'd have called me in by now, she reasoned, swaying slightly under Noah's insistent gaze. *Wilson doesn't know a thing, and that weird guy was just homeless. I'm totally in the clear.*

Probably.

She had to admit she wasn't anxious to test that theory.

On the other hand, Noah did outrank her. If she followed his orders and they got in trouble, he'd be the one to take the heat.

Probably.

"All right. Fine!" she said, giving in. "You want to go? We'll go."

"That's my girl," Noah told her with a conspiratorial grin. "Get ready to rock Owen Vincent's world."

* * *

If someone looks out a window and sees us, they'll call the cops for sure, Sydney worried as she and

Noah jogged the two long, hot blocks to SST. He had moved the van closer, but parking on SpaceSoft property was out of the question—there was always the chance they would need to get away quickly. *Coveralls, leather gloves . . . yeah, we look normal. Wait until they see the ski masks.*

She felt the lump in her front pocket, making sure the mask Noah had given her hadn't fallen out. She would have preferred to walk in wearing normal clothes and trying to act natural, but they couldn't risk having their faces show up on security tapes, which was why they were headed for a side door that didn't have an outside camera. The only saving grace was that the surrounding streets and parking lots were deserted that Sunday morning, a modern-day ghost town of glass and concrete.

The side of the SST tower was only feet away when Noah took his ski mask from his pocket and pulled it on still running, motioning for her to do the same. Then he took out a ring of keys and fit one into a metal door used by maintenance workers. The door swung open. They were in.

"The lab's on fifteen," Noah whispered, leading the way down a dingy hall. "We'll take the freight elevator."

Sydney stuck close behind him, looking nervously about, but there was no sign of a security guard or anyone else in the building. They made it into the big steel-walled elevator unobserved.

"We'll do this the way we discussed in the van," Noah whispered on the way up. "And the less talking, the better. Just in case."

Sydney nodded, her adrenaline starting to kick in. The only bugs they had found around SST so far were their own, but there was no point in taking chances.

The freight elevator stopped. Noah grinned through the little hole in his mask. "Let's do this thing," he said.

They stepped out on the fifteenth floor, and Sydney immediately realized that this part of the building was different. The small lobby in front of the elevator was walled entirely in steel and bounded on both sides by solid metal doors blocking off the hallways.

"This can't be good," she said apprehensively.

But Noah headed straight for the door on their left. "I told you these labs were a little tougher," he reminded her in a whisper.

The entry system on the security door was a standard keypad device with a card slot. An authorized person inserted a magnetized card and keyed in the appropriate code, causing the door to slide open automatically. Noah wasn't an authorized person. He took a rubber-handled screwdriver from his pocket and rammed its metal end into the slot, shorting out the wiring. Smoke filtered up through the keypad; the lights on the unit went dead.

"Come on!" he whispered, motioning for Sydney to help him with the heavy door.

At first the slick surface gave them no purchase; no matter how they pushed, the door remained motionless. At last they got it rolling, though, and once a crack was opened they were able to grab the door's edge and pull it back the rest of the way. Noah wedged his screwdriver under the bottom to keep it from rolling shut.

"What if we need that again?" Sydney whispered, pointing to the tool.

"What if we need to get out?"

Leaving the screwdriver behind, they started down a windowless hallway, Sydney's pulse racing faster with every step. Turning on SST, betraying people she knew and had worked with, was far more nerve-racking than hitting a neutral place.

A hundred feet down the hall, Noah stopped in front of a recessed doorway. The metal door barring this entrance also had a security pad, but instead of a keyed code and card, this one required a palm scan.

"Crap," Noah said under his breath. "This has got to be the only one of these in the building."

Sydney's misgivings rushed back as she realized Noah hadn't fully anticipated the lab's security measures. "Can you fake it somehow?" she whispered.

"I'll give it a try," he said, pulling off one glove. Sticking his tongue through his mask, he licked the palm of his hand and placed it on the scan pad.

"Gross!"

"Don't get squeamish on me now," he muttered, rotating his palm slightly as the beam began to scan. He kept his hand barely moving, hoping to trick the machine into reading his lines in the right places, but when the scan was complete, a single red word was displayed: DENIED.

"Okay," he said, dropping his hand and taking a few steps back. "New plan."

The side kick he leveled at the security pad was so forceful that Sydney felt its vibrations through her feet. The pad sheared off the wall, dangling crazily by a few wires. Noah yanked the pad off completely and began crossing the exposed wires. A moment later, she heard something click.

"Open the door," he said, still holding two wires together.

She sprang forward and grabbed the doorknob. The lock had disengaged; the door swung open easily. "We're in!" she whispered.

"Did you doubt it?"

"That's rhetorical, right?"

Noah rolled his eyes as he walked past her into the lab. Following just behind, Sydney saw a long, antiseptically white room humming with computers. There were no windows, no other doors, not so much as a scrap of paper lying out on one of the tables. Computers, associated furniture, lights, and a security camera were the only things in the room. And then Noah pushed a panel in the back wall aside and Sydney saw the safe.

"Here's where I need you to be my lookout," he whispered, using his gloved left hand to stretch the bare fingers of his right. "This shouldn't take *too* long."

She nodded but didn't move, wanting to watch him work. Noah's fingertips closed lightly around the combination dial of the black wall-mounted vault. He pressed his ear to its metal surface and began spinning the knob slowly, his eyes dropping closed to increase his concentration. The technique he was using relied on feeling the way the dial moved, mentally cataloging the places it spun freely or slowed or clicked to figure out the position of the safe's tumblers and, ultimately, the combination. Noah was an expert at safe manipulation, but the process took focus—and in a big room with only one exit he would be vulnerable the entire time his attention was off the door.

Tearing herself away, Sydney headed back to the lab entrance. If anyone showed up on the fifteenth floor, she wanted to know in plenty of time to warn Noah and get them both out of there. She moved cautiously into the doorway alcove, then eased her head into the hallway and looked in both directions. There was no sign of another person, and unlike the thickly carpeted hallways downstairs, the hallways on fifteen were surfaced with a hard, echo-prone linoleum. She ought to be able to hear footsteps before anyone got too close. Pulling back into the alcove, Sydney leaned against a side wall and prepared to wait.

The nervous sweat she had broken on her way up to the lab turned gradually cold and clammy as she fidgeted in her hiding place, wondering what was taking Noah so long. Back in the van, he'd assured her that the safe wasn't high-tech and he'd be into it fairly quickly, but now, with nothing to do but wait for something to go wrong, every second she stood there felt like a week. Her heart fluttered with dread, and when an air-conditioning unit clicked on overhead, she nearly jumped out of her coveralls.

Minute after slow minute crept by. They had

gone too far to bail out now, but every second they stayed in the building increased their chances of being caught. If they didn't get out soon . . .

Sydney couldn't take it anymore. With one last check of the hallway, she hurried back to Noah.

"What's going on?" she whispered.

"Shhh!" he whispered back, every muscle in his body tensing. "I've practically got it."

"What if someone comes?"

"That's *your* job," he reminded her, still working the dial. "Just give me another second. . . ." His fingers stopped abruptly. "There! I think that's it."

Taking his ear off the safe, Noah moved his hand to the door latch. "Feeling lucky?" he asked her, giving the handle a twist.

The door opened on the first try.

In the exact center of the safe sat a portable hard drive, like a pearl in an oversized oyster. Sydney reached for it eagerly, knowing the intel it contained could change history.

Noah was right to break in, she realized. *If the bad guys had gotten here first, stealing this program would have been just as easy for them.*

Her hand closed over the paperback-book-sized device. She lifted it out of the safe—and set off a piercing alarm.

Wailing echoed off the white walls, so loud it

seemed to be inside her head. She almost dropped the drive to cover her ears, cringing in pain when she realized she couldn't do either.

Noah grabbed the hard drive from her, stuffing it into his coveralls. "Run!" he yelled, pushing her toward the door.

Sydney ran, her sneakers slipping on the linoleum. Tearing out of the lab, she bounced off the opposite wall and sprinted toward the elevator. The alarm was even more excruciating in the hallway. She curled her arms around her head, trying to protect her eardrums. She'd never heard such a deafening sound; her skull felt about to explode.

The door up ahead was still wedged open with Noah's screwdriver. But, to Sydney's amazement, it was slowly closing anyway, forcing the screwdriver backward over the metal threshold in a shower of small sparks.

Security override, she realized, running full tilt. Whatever she'd set off was trying to lock them in the building. Panicked, she glanced back over her shoulder. Noah was well behind, but running fast. He'd make it through the door.

Clearing the threshold, Sydney dashed straight to the freight elevator. To her relief, it was still on their floor, its doors wide open. Running inside, she pushed the button for the ground floor; Noah would be there any second and she wanted to speed their exit. But the instant she touched the button, something terrible happened. The doors didn't close with the customary gentle laziness of elevators; they slammed shut like a vault. Sydney glimpsed Noah's horrified face through the narrowing gap as he came around the corner and realized what she'd done.

"No! Stairs!" he cried, lunging forward.

But he was too late. The doors had shut tight between them.

"It's locked up!" she screamed over the siren, frantically pressing buttons. None of them worked anymore.

"I'll get the screwdriver," he yelled back.

A moment later, she heard him prying at the joint between the doors.

"You have to go!" she shouted. "Get out with the intel!"

Dropping the screwdriver, Noah gave the doors an angry kick. They didn't even budge. The siren was still wailing.

"Okay," she thought she heard him say. Then nothing.

"Okay?" Sydney pressed her ear to the crack. "Noah? Noah, are you out there?"

Nothing but the wailing of the siren.

He left me! she realized, stumbling backward. Even though she'd told him to, she'd never thought he would. *How am I supposed to get out of here now?*

She glanced frantically around the elevator's metal interior, but there was no place to hide. The buttons were still locked. She spotted what might be an emergency trapdoor in the ceiling near one corner, but it was too high to reach.

The siren stopped abruptly, the quiet it left behind so intense that Sydney couldn't hear anything except the ringing in her ears. She slumped with relief, just for a moment.

And then she heard boots running down the hallway. A security team was coming, and it was headed in her direction.

Think, Sydney. Think! she exhorted herself.

A handrail wrapped three sides of the elevator car. It only protruded six inches, but there was a chance she could use it to climb to the ceiling, getting the leverage she needed by placing her feet on adjoining walls near the corner.

The racket of boots was growing louder. Trembling, breathing in shallow little gasps, Sydney put her right sneaker on the railing and jumped with her left leg, trying to bridge the corner and catch a second foothold. She missed, barking her shin on the way down. Another try; another failure. There was so much noise in the hall she could hardly think.

The third time she tried, her left foot caught the railing. She teetered in space a moment, her hands grasping empty air. Then she threw her weight forward and braced herself on the corner walls. Her head nearly touched the ceiling. Not wasting a moment, she pushed hard on the panel above her. It popped up and out, revealing a small escape hatch.

I did it! she thought. *Now if I can get through there without falling . . .*

The angle was awkward and she was trembling so hard she could barely control her limbs, but somehow she got her hands, then her forearms up over the edges of the opening, the rest of her body dangling beneath her. A few properly timed kicks later, she had pulled herself out onto the elevator's dusty roof. Hurriedly, she replaced the panel, eliminating the last trace of her presence. Then she crouched in the darkness of the elevator shaft, waiting for her knees to stop shaking.

The elevator doors opened beneath her.

"It's clear!" someone shouted.

The doors closed again. She was safe.

For the moment.

They'll check here eventually. I've got to get out of the building.

She could still hear the security squad running around, searching for intruders. Every second she delayed made her capture more likely. Looking up toward the top of the shaft, Sydney saw a glimmer of light.

If I could climb one of these elevator cables to the roof, I might be able to get out where that light's coming in, she thought. *There have to be fire escapes down the outside of the building.*

It wouldn't have been her first choice, especially since the roof was eight stories up, but it was the only option she saw. Grabbing a thick steel cable firmly between her gloved hands, Sydney began to climb.

At first, she forced herself not to look up, knowing the distance above her head could only discourage her. Instead, she focused on pulling smoothly with her arms, using her legs to help her climb. The thick leather gloves Noah had provided were a blessing to her now, and the coveralls, although hot in the stuffy shaft, protected her legs from the cable.

Just keep going. One floor at a time, she told herself determinedly.

But it didn't take long before her arms began trembling and her shoulders had knotted painfully.

Each pull got harder and harder, until she could barely keep from crying out. *Just a little farther. A little farther . . .*

And then she looked up.

I'll never make it! She was only halfway up, and her entire body quivered from the strain of holding on. But she had no choice; she had to keep going.

She had just begun to climb again, calling up her last reserves of strength, when something clanked loudly overhead. The cable jerked to life, burning upward through her gloved palms. The elevator was in motion, headed for the roof. Sydney slid down as the car traveled up, its roof getting closer and closer.

Timing her release as well as she could, she let go of the cable ten feet above the car's roof. It flew up underneath her, hitting her feet with a breathtaking thud. She collapsed into a heap on the moving car.

Anyone inside had to have heard that. But no voices sounded beneath her. The car was apparently empty.

Scrambling into a crouch, Sydney looked up. She was almost to the building's roof. And now she saw the dangerous machinery overhead, coming toward her out of the gloom. An enormous pulley system powered the car's rapid rise, and she was about to be pulled right into it.

Her heart was beating triple speed. There was no time left to think. Spotting a narrow ledge in the shaft wall, Sydney gathered her courage and leaped.

Her toes and face slammed into the wall. She teetered on the steel I beam that formed the ledge, barely hanging on as the car rushed past her toward the roof. The wind it made nearly sucked her backward off her perch, but somehow she held on, flattening herself against the shaft wall as the car reversed direction and rushed back down. She heard it rumbling far below before she opened her eyes again.

The wall of the shaft she clung to was made of steel beams placed at regular intervals with vertical columns tying them together. A mishmash of pipes and conduits ran across this surface, providing a few more handholds. If she fell, she was dead. But she could see the source of the light now: a short, horizontal shaft a mere eight feet above her.

Taking a deep breath, Sydney began to climb. A minute later, she had pulled herself into a ventilation shaft and was thrilled to see open rooftop on the other side of a flimsy grill.

I made it! she thought ecstatically, kicking her

way through the grill. She wriggled out of the shaft, blinking in the bright sunshine. Then she hurried to the edge of the roof and looked over the side of the building in search of a fire escape.

What she saw instead nearly took her breath away. The street in front of SST swarmed with police and security vehicles. An impossible number of officers filled the parking lot. She couldn't possibly escape down the front of the building.

She was wheeling around to sprint for the back wall when an unpleasantly familiar noise caught her attention—the whir of helicopter rotors. The aircraft was circling in from the north, its pilot certain to spot her any moment.

Sydney glanced at the parking lot again, paralyzed by indecision. She hadn't the slightest chance of getting through the police barricade. But the helicopter was flying closer by the second. Even if she found a way down the back of the building, she'd never make it to the ground without the pilot's seeing her.

The truth she'd been denying ever since the freight elevator had slammed shut hit her like a revelation.

She was trapped. She was exposed. And she was all out of options.

My career as a spy is over.

![Chapter 11]

IT CAN'T BE OVER, Sydney thought desperately. *Not now. Not like this.*

Wilson's hopes for her future had been so high. Her own had been even higher. She had joined the CIA because she wanted to help her country, to make a difference. If she was exposed as a secret agent, she might still be able to do that—but not in SD-6.

The thought galvanized her. Charging back to the ventilation shaft, Sydney dove into its opening. Her coveralls slid along the slick metal surface, catapulting her forward. For a moment she was airborne. . . .

Then her hands closed around an elevator cable, holding on with more strength than she'd known she had. Her legs swung through space. One of her knees kinked around the cable and she eased her grip, sliding down the shaft like a fireman on a pole. When she finally spotted the elevator car at rest on the ground floor, she knew what she was going to do.

If I could get beneath that car, no one would ever find me. There had to be some sort of dead space; the elevator couldn't slam the ground every time it went to the bottom. Moments later her feet touched the car's roof, quietly this time, and she let go of the cable.

No voices came from inside the car. Sydney crept to its edge, looking for a way down. The car itself offered no handholds, but there was a good crossbeam on the shaft wall. Taking careful aim, she jumped across the gap.

Her hands closed on the beam, her feet scrabbled onto a pipe, and immediately she began climbing down. Her body was on autopilot now, doing what it knew how to do, what it had been trained to do, taking her brain along for the ride. She cleared the car and released her grip, dropping the final few feet to the bottom of the shaft.

Sydney landed in a crouch on the concrete floor of a pit so dark she could barely see. She held her breath, listening to her own pounding heart, until she could make out a subterranean room only slightly bigger than the elevator car. As she had surmised, large cylindrical shock absorbers kept the bottom of the elevator a few feet off the floor. Rising tentatively, she moved cautiously forward to explore this cramped space.

There was no sound at all from up above. The pit's concrete walls were soundproof, and the motionless car formed a low roof over her head. She was considering staying there overnight, then sneaking back into the elevator and walking out of the building disguised as a janitor on Monday morning, when she came upon a door.

ELEVATOR REPAIR ACCESS—EXIT, said a red-lettered sign. Below that was a deadbolt allowing the door to be unlocked from Sydney's side. For a long moment she just stood there, afraid of setting off another alarm. Then she reached out and flipped the bolt, yanking the door open in nearly the same motion.

Light flooded the elevator pit, dazzling her eyes. The exit had opened into a masonry-lined outdoor shaft three feet square with metal ladder rungs leading up to ground level. She could see a low brick wall to keep people from falling in, and above that, bushes and blue sky. She was outside and, so far, unobserved.

Sydney stripped off her ski mask, coveralls, and gloves, tossing them back into the pit before letting the access door close behind her. She hesitated nervously at the bottom of the ladder, smoothing her ponytail, making sure her shorts and tank top looked clean, and weighing her limited options. Then, grabbing the first rung, she climbed slowly to the top, every nerve stretched for the first sign of danger.

She had emerged on the side of the building she and Noah had entered. The distance between her and the street was short, and, to her amazement, the street was deserted. She could hear shouts and sirens from in front and in back of the building, but no one was watching this side. Even the helicopter was out of sight. Stepping out over the low brick wall, Sydney squared her shoulders and began walking toward the street.

Don't run. Don't rush. Don't even hurry, she cautioned herself as she went. If anyone spotted her, she wanted to look like a lost college girl, not a person with something to hide. It took every bit of self-possession to keep her stride to a saunter and her ponytail swinging behind her, but she made it to the sidewalk undetected.

Every step increases my chances, she thought, continuing straight across the street. No one at SST knew what she really looked like, and she wasn't carrying a single incriminating thing. *I can make it. I'm almost safe.*

On the other side of the street, a row of oleanders formed a loose hedge along the sidewalk. Sydney glanced back over her shoulder. The ruckus at SST was starting to come into view, but no one was looking her way. Cutting between the bushes, she walked down a plant-covered slope into the parking lot of another office building. A few scattered cars were parked in its spaces, and Sydney heaved a sigh of relief. If she had to, she could pretend one of the cars was hers and that she'd lost her keys somehow. But each passing second made the need for a cover story less likely, and at this new lower level, she was out of sight of everything but the helicopter.

I wonder where it is, she worried. If the aircraft had landed somewhere, she was safe. But if it was still circling . . .

"Took you long enough!" a loud voice said.

Sydney whipped around, only to find Noah

grinning at her from inside his janitor's van, which was peeking out from behind a brick Dumpster enclosure.

"Hurry up," he urged out the driver's window. "The chopper's not flying at the moment, and I'd like to get out of here."

Sydney didn't need to be asked twice. Running to the van, she climbed in on the passenger side. Noah started the engine and began driving away, keeping the van's speed low to avoid attracting attention.

"I can't believe you waited!" she said.

"What did you think?" he asked. "That I was going to abandon you?"

Yes, actually.

But looking at him now, she didn't want to admit that. His whole face glowed with the thrill of a mission accomplished, and his body rocked back and forth as he drove, letting off excess steam.

"Was that a rush or what?" he exclaimed. "We make a serious team."

Sydney shook her head, still trying to process this unexpected turn of events. "How did you even know which way I'd be leaving the building?"

Noah gave her an incredulous look. "You were stuck in the freight elevator. Where else were you going to come out? Not on the roof, that's for sure."

The possibility that she might not get out at all apparently hadn't occurred to him—and she liked that, she realized. She liked that a lot.

"No . . .not the roof . . . ," she murmured. "Obviously bad."

Noah steered around a corner, putting a little more distance between them and SST.

"I am pumped!" he announced, slapping the steering wheel. "Nothing's better than pulling off something like that! Using your wits, your training . . ." He turned to her again, his eyes shining with excitement. "Admit it. Wasn't that the most fun you've had all week?"

Sydney's jaw dropped. She searched for the words to tell him how crazy he was, but somehow the outrage wouldn't come.

For the first time in days she felt back in control—strong, capable, powerful . . . not to mention smarter than the average thief. She and Noah had just faced the impossible and totally kicked its butt.

"Yes," she said at last, feeling his satisfied grin spread to her face. "Today was the most fun by far."

"Stick with me," he advised her, winking. "I know what you need."

* * *

"Let me see it," Sydney demanded in the SD-6 elevator.

Noah handed over the portable hard drive they'd just stolen, and for the second time that day she held it in her hands. She studied the drive intently, willing its exterior to give up some clue to the importance of its data, but the beige plastic case was completely generic. Its only unique feature was a teensy blue dot on one side, as if an uncapped pen had bumped against it at some point. She licked her thumb and rubbed the plastic, but the mark was permanent.

"Impressive, isn't it?" Noah said, holding out his hand for it.

Sydney gave the drive back. She would have liked to be the one to carry the program triumphantly into Wilson's office. Except . . . should they really give it to Wilson?

"Noah?" she said, just as the elevator doors opened.

He walked into the small white transition room. "What?"

But she couldn't bring herself to tell him she'd been spying on her handler. She didn't have a good enough reason, and she hadn't seen one incriminating thing. Besides, if she'd wanted to talk about it, she should have brought it up before now.

"Nothing," she said, stepping up to have her retinas scanned.

To Sydney's relief, Wilson was every bit as ecstatic as Noah had predicted, jumping out of his seat when he heard the news.

"I can't believe it!" he exclaimed. "You've got the program? Are you sure?"

"Right here," Noah said proudly, handing over the hard drive.

Wilson took the drive in a state of amazement, barely glancing at its case. "I can't believe you just went in there and stole it! Why didn't you call me for backup?" This last was directed at Sydney.

Uh-oh. She shifted nervously in her sneakers, trying to think of a good answer. "We wanted to," she began, "but—"

"Never mind. Doesn't matter," Wilson interrupted. "I can't wait to get this to Graham for analysis."

"I'll take it," she offered quickly. It seemed she was off the hook—both for freelancing in the park and for her wild ride with Noah—but she wouldn't mind leaving her boss's office before he changed his mind. Besides, it would be fun to see Graham's face when he heard how they'd spanked SST.

"He's not in," Wilson said. "I'll have to call him."

"Oh."

"You know what? I'm going to take this to Op-Tech myself and wait for him there," Wilson said. "He's usually here in ten minutes, and I'm anxious to get started."

"You want us to hang out?" Noah asked.

"No, go on home. Take a couple days off," Wilson said. "You too, Sydney. You've earned it."

"Really? You don't need me?" she asked, surprised. "You're sure?"

"Of course we *need* you," he said with a smile, "but we'll muddle through until Wednesday."

"And I'm not going back to SST either? I mean, just to be sure . . ."

Wilson laughed. "I'd give SST a wide berth if I were you, at least until we get this wrapped up."

"Right. Okay, then," she said, still stunned. If Wilson didn't watch out, she might actually get caught up in her classes.

Wilson started to step past her on his way to Op-Tech, then abruptly stopped. His eyes met hers and held them, as if he had something to say. She leaned toward him intently, willing him to spit it out. His hand patted her shoulder.

"I'm so proud of you, Sydney," he said huskily. And then he strode off down the hall.

She stared after him, both amazed and touched.

Just a few words, but they meant so much. All her unfounded suspicions vanished on a sigh. Wilson would never be able to say so, but he loved her like family; she'd just read it in his face. He'd never do anything to hurt her or SD-6.

"Ooh, teacher's pet!" Noah gave her a playful shove. "How come he's not proud of *me*?"

"Maybe because you're already so proud of yourself," she suggested, shoving back.

"Watch it," he said, assuming an exaggerated wrestling stance. "Because I can totally take you."

"You wish. Pound for pound, I'd wipe the floor with you."

"I'm waiting to see you try."

Sydney did her best to stare him down, but the goofy look on Noah's face totally cracked her up.

"What's gotten into you?" she asked, laughing. "If you're not more careful, people might start believing you can actually stand me."

He pursed his lips, thinking it over. "You're not completely intolerable."

"That's it!" she exclaimed, barely able to keep from kissing him right there. "Let's settle this in the garage."

12

"HI, GRAHAM," SYDNEY SAID, peeking into his workroom Monday afternoon. SD-6's gadget genius was bent over a piece of circuitry, a soldering iron in one hand and a pair of bug-eyed magnifiers strapped around his head. "How's it going?"

"Sydney!" he said, jumping up. He did a shocked double take, then remembered the magnifiers, nearly burning his face with the soldering iron in his struggle to remove them. "I didn't expect to see you here today."

"I know," she said, smiling wryly. "Wilson finally gives me a day off, and I come in anyway. I just couldn't stand being out of the loop on this SST thing. The joke's on me, though, because Wilson's not even here."

Graham seemed surprised. "He was here a few minutes ago."

"Well, he's not in his office and I can't find him, so I thought I'd visit you."

"Sure! Hey, have a seat."

Equipment scattered everywhere as Graham dropped his soldering iron and dumped half a dozen things from his rolling chair onto the floor. He brushed the upholstery with his hand, trying to make it more presentable, then wheeled the chair toward Sydney.

"You don't have to go to so much trouble," she murmured, embarrassed. She didn't even want to sit down, but the eager look on his face would have made it cruel not to. "I just wanted to ask how it went with the missile program. Is it as dangerous as we expected?"

Graham looked stunned. "You didn't hear?"

"Hear what?"

"That disk you guys brought me was garbage. I'm not blaming *you*," he added quickly, reading the horrified look on her face. "Agent Hicks might have been confused about what got put in that safe. Or Vincent could have locked up a decoy. Or it's possible some kind of security pulse corrupted the data when you snatched it. . . ."

Graham leaned against his overflowing desk, his gaze focused on empty space. "Except that a pulse usually wipes clean, and I've never seen so much digital junk."

"Are you certain?" Sydney asked disbelievingly. "It's not just encoded?"

"Huh?" His eyes snapped back to hers. "Oh, code. That's what we all thought at first. The thing is, I'm pretty good at code. Not that I'm bragging, but—"

Sydney had stopped listening. Her stomach felt like it was back on top of that freight elevator.

"This is a nightmare!" she cried. "You don't know what we went through to get that thing. We can't go back there, and even if we could, the software's been moved by now. The program, all the data . . . Owen's not stupid. We may never find it again."

"No, Owen Vincent isn't stupid," Graham agreed, ignoring everything else she'd just said. "You know, for a while I thought that data was some kind of worm, and if I could just grab one end of it, the program would unravel like a sweater."

Worms? Sweaters?

"Huh?"

"Did you ever see that Stephen King movie?

Everyone thinks Jack Nicholson's writing a play, but really he's just in his room typing page after page of 'All work and no play makes Jack a dull boy.'" Graham paused, wrinkling his brow. "I think that's what he was typing. Anyhow, the point is, there was never a play to begin with—only a bunch of garbage. I thought maybe if I could crack into your disk at just the right place, all that data might line up somehow. It could be a repetitive string. Something like 'Not hiring Graham Flinkman was the biggest mistake of my career.'"

"Yes, I'm sure that's what it would say." Sydney forced a fleeting smile. "Can I see it?"

"See what?" he asked, confused. "There's nothing to see. I was just—"

"I mean the hard drive we stole. What happened to it?"

"Oh. It's around here somewhere," he said, turning to dig through a pile of components. "Wilson wanted me to lock it up when I finished, but, well . . . there's no rush now." Graham located the device at last and handed it to Sydney.

"Sorry," he said sympathetically. "Better luck next time."

"Thanks."

She gazed down at the hard drive in her hands, not even sure why she'd asked to see it. It was just so disappointing to risk so much and have it be for nothing. For all she knew, the real software had already been sold, and SD-6 wouldn't find out who'd bought it until missiles started hitting the wrong targets. She blinked hard against frustrated tears, the drive swimming in and out of focus. She hated its bland plastic case, its complete lack of any identifying—

"Hey!" she said, suddenly. "Hey, this is the wrong drive!"

Graham shook his head. "That's the one Wilson gave me."

"No, it isn't."

"Yes, it is."

"No! Because the one I gave him—"

Sydney cut herself off in midsentence, unsure whether to continue. Should she tell Graham about the blue mark? Because the case in her hands didn't have one.

This is not *the drive I gave Wilson!* She had never been more certain of anything, and her mind reeled to think what it meant. The only reasonable conclusion was that the device she'd stolen was someplace else—and that it had made its disappearance after she'd entrusted it to her boss.

Graham was staring at her, waiting for her to continue.

"Oh, wait. This *is* it," she said sheepishly. "My mistake."

Graham smiled, relieved, and took it back.

"I'd better get going," she said, standing up. "I'm meeting someone for dinner soon."

"Okay. See you Wednesday."

"Yes. Wednesday."

Sydney headed for the elevator, still in shock. She regretted lying to Graham, but she felt sure she'd done the right thing. If she couldn't even trust her own handler, how could she trust some guy she barely knew?

How can I trust anyone?

* * *

Sydney drove out of the SD-6 parking garage and onto the busy downtown street without a destination in mind. She had been so excited about seeing Wilson and hearing him tell her again what a great job she'd done. That the disk would turn out to be useless was the last thing she'd expected.

Because it wasn't *useless,* she thought. *Why else would it have disappeared?*

Her head ached with possibilities, none of them good. She navigated traffic in a daze, barely seeing the other cars.

This is the worst. And I can't believe I have to meet my dad in an hour!

She had actually been happy about it when he'd called earlier that day, inviting her to dinner. But, as usual, his timing had proved to be awful. She was already dressed for the restaurant, having planned to head there straight from her visit with Wilson, but she'd left before she'd expected and it was too early to go there now.

I'll just drive around. Kill some time.

She certainly had plenty to think about, and it wouldn't hurt to compose herself before she met her father. But it wasn't long before she realized she was headed straight for the house in the suburbs she'd followed Wilson to before. Whether or not the house was his, it was the only place she knew to look. And if she found him there . . .

Why not? she thought, perking up. *Why not just ask him what happened to the hard drive? There's probably some perfectly good explanation.*

She relaxed in her seat, feeling better already. Wilson would explain, she'd have dinner with her father, and tomorrow she'd catch up on the rest of her schoolwork.

Everything was going to be fine.

But before she was cruising the final blocks, she'd started worrying again. If she did find Wilson, he'd want to know how she'd done it. And if she didn't . . .

Up ahead, at the intersection, a black SUV passed from left to right. Sydney's heart raced as she recognized her boss in the driver's seat. She held her breath, willing him not to look her way. . . .

He didn't.

Here we go, she thought, making a right turn. *Freelancing: The Sequel.*

Dusk was lengthening the shadows as Sydney followed Wilson into downtown Hollywood. Some cars had turned on their headlights, but most continued without them. Traffic snarled to a crawl, moving bumper to bumper. Trailing a block behind the SUV, terrified of being seen, Sydney welcomed the increased cover.

Where is he going? she wondered as they passed the heart of the tourist district and headed into less upscale surroundings.

Seedy bars and clubs were thick on both sides of the street before Wilson finally pulled to the curb and started feeding a parking meter.

Sydney cranked her steering wheel hard to the right, driving into an alley. Locking up her Mustang, praying it would still be there when she got back, she pulled on her black blazer and hurried to follow Wilson.

She didn't spot him right away, and for a moment, she nearly panicked. People streamed in and out of a dozen doorways, wandering from bar to bar. Wilson could have walked into any of them, and she didn't even have her SD-6 fake ID. Then a man caught her eye a block farther on, making her weak with relief. Wilson was walking away from her down the sidewalk, a fast food bag in one hand.

When did he stop for dinner? she wondered, zeroing in on the white paper bag. *If there's food in that bag, it has to be stone cold.*

She followed cautiously, keeping one eye on the suspicious bag. Her black jacket and the gathering darkness made her feel a little safer, but she still dreaded the thought of his turning around. Wilson walked through a swath of light outside an open doorway, dodging a couple of times to avoid other pedestrians. Then, twenty feet into the darkness on the other side, his left hand flicked toward a trash can and came back empty.

The fast food bag was gone.

It's a drop!

Sydney's pulse pounded with the realization. Wilson hadn't driven all the way to Hollywood just to get rid of his trash. Ducking into a doorway, she let him walk on without her, her eyes riveted to the concrete trash receptacle by the side of the road.

And suddenly she remembered the homeless man in the park. If he was Wilson's contact, he could come along any second, pretending to scavenge for food. No one would look twice. In this neighborhood, no one would look once.

Without another thought, Sydney bolted forward. Snatching the bag from the trash, she opened its crumpled top and yanked out its contents—a portable hard drive like the one she'd stolen from SST, complete with a teensy blue dot.

No.

She stood immobilized, unable to process the information. Passersby flowed around her like water around a stone.

If Wilson gave Graham a bad drive, and he's dropping the good one for somebody else . . .

No.

It couldn't be.

But it couldn't be anything else. The man she'd trusted with her life was leaking the CIA's secrets to the enemy.

A tear rolled down Sydney's cheek, the start of a heart-wrenching ache taking over her whole body.

Wilson's a double agent.

To: tchristian@cia.gov

From: rlw@free-mailboxes.com

Subject: SST

Have completed drop per your instructions. Confirm receipt and arrange earliest possible extraction. Suspect SD-6 surveillance. Would obviously prefer to get out alive.

13

I CAN'T JUST STAND here.

The thought cut through the haze in Sydney's brain, forcing her to concentrate on something besides the pain of Wilson's betrayal. People continued to pass her on the sidewalk, but that was no guarantee of safety. Whoever Wilson was working for, it wasn't the CIA, and that meant she was in danger.

I should go after him, she thought, paralyzed.

Maybe if she confronted him, he'd still be able to explain.

Explain what? she thought bitterly. *What could he possibly say? I have the evidence right in my hands!*

And if he had no chance of justifying his actions, she had even less of bringing him down by force. Wilson was a big man, extremely well trained, and very probably armed. The deadliest weapon she was carrying was her car keys. What was to keep him from just shooting her?

He wouldn't.

But she wasn't sure of that anymore. She wasn't sure of anything.

I could be standing in somebody's sights right now.

Torn, confused, and late to meet her father, Sydney tucked the hard drive into her blazer pocket, turned around, and ran.

* * *

By the time she parked her car outside the restaurant, Sydney had achieved an outward appearance of calm. The tears she'd cried driving across town had dried, and even the ache of her loss had dulled, replaced by a growing anger. Wilson had betrayed her. He'd betrayed them all. And as soon as she got through dinner, she'd decide what to do about that.

Assuming my dad even waited, she thought, running up to the entry. She was almost an hour late and fully expecting a tongue-lashing if he was still there.

The front door of the steak house was standing open. Sydney hurried through it, craning her neck past a giant fish tank in an attempt to see the tables. There weren't many diners that Monday night, and her father sat conspicuously alone, a menu and cup of coffee in front of him.

"Can I help you?" a hostess asked, quickly inserting herself between Sydney and the dining room. She was young and nervous-looking, her long hair gathered into a loose ponytail down the back of her Hawaiian-print dress.

"That gray-haired man," Sydney said, pointing at her father. "How long has he been here waiting?"

The girl turned to look. "Five minutes. Ten at the most."

"That's not possible!" Sydney protested.

"I seated him myself."

"Oh. Well, okay. If you're sure . . ."

But she still found it inconceivable that her obsessively punctual father had been almost as late as she was. What had he been doing?

If he gives me a hard time, at least I have ammunition, she thought, heading toward his table.

I'm not even going to make up an excuse. In fact, I dare him to ask why I'm late.

But Jack simply nodded as she approached, as if she were right on time. "Hello, Sydney. Did you have trouble finding this place?"

"Maybe a little," she said warily. "Did you?"

"Of course not. I'm the one who suggested it."

"Right."

He looked expectantly from her to the empty seat on the other side of his table. She sat down on cue, nervously picking up the menu lying there.

"Have you ordered yet?" she asked.

"No, I was waiting for you."

You weren't waiting very long. But she kept the thought to herself. She had enough problems already without picking a fight. "What's good here?" she asked instead.

"The steak. And the seafood."

"Uh-huh. Pretty much everything on the menu, then."

"Exactly." If he'd noticed her sarcasm, he didn't let on.

A waitress walked over. "Can I bring you something from the bar?" she asked Sydney.

"Sadly, no."

"We'll order dinner now," Jack said. "Do you have a special tonight?"

"We have three," the woman replied, gearing up for a lengthy description. "Our first is the almond-crusted halibut with—"

"I'll have that," he said.

The waitress blinked. "You don't want to hear the other two?"

"That's not necessary."

"Um, soup or salad?"

"Salad. House dressing," he said brusquely.

"All right." The woman turned her attention to Sydney. "Also tonight, we have a seared—"

"I'll have the halibut too," Sydney said, putting down her unread menu. The sooner she got out of there, the better. "House dressing."

The waitress walked away shaking her head.

"I'm sorry if I seem rushed, but something's come up at work," Jack told Sydney. "I'm afraid I'll have to eat and run tonight."

"I thought you were on vacation."

He shrugged. "I just have to make some calls. Clients . . . you know. Sometimes it takes concessions to keep them happy."

"Concessions. Right," she said, seething inside.

Who was he to talk to her about concessions? Wasn't she sitting with him in a restaurant she hadn't wanted to go to, waiting for a meal she didn't want to eat, while a dangerous double agent ran wild and a hard drive full of missile software rotted in her purse?

But forget all that. No, we're cutting dinner short tonight because one of Jack Bristow's precious clients desperately needs a wing nut.

The situation was almost too ridiculous.

How did I ever start believing that what I do is important? she wondered sullenly. *Dad's got a big-time career selling airplane parts, and I'm just trying to save the world.*

* * *

"Thanks for coming," Sydney said, stepping out of a shadow behind the UCLA gym.

Noah flinched, startled, then tried to pretend he hadn't. Darkness cloaked the surrounding athletic fields, but a security light on the building made reading his face easy.

"No problem," he said, joining her in a sheltered alcove. "Now tell me what's so important you couldn't say it on the phone."

"Just . . ." Sydney hesitated. She'd had a lot of time to think while she'd pushed that halibut around her plate, while she'd driven back to campus, and while she'd waited for Noah to show up. What if, in spite of everything, she was wrong about Wilson?

"Oh, I get it," he said smugly, pulling her into his arms. "You want *me*. It's not in my job description, but I'll try to be of service, ma'am."

"You wish." Sydney pushed him off her, in no mood for his jokes. She hesitated another second, then blurted it out. "Something terrible's happened, Noah. I don't know what to do."

His expression changed immediately, becoming completely serious. "Tell me."

"Look." Pulling the hard drive from her bag, Sydney handed it over. "Check out the mark on that side. That's the drive—the exact drive—you and I stole from SST."

Noah held the case close to his eyes and squinted. "If you say so. But why do you have it? Did Graham give this to you?"

"No. Wilson dropped it into a trash can on a Hollywood street tonight. I thought . . ." The lump in her throat had begun choking her. "He's been acting funny, so I started following him around. And now . . ." She gestured helplessly to the disk.

Noah's face told her all she needed to know. This was serious—as serious as she'd feared.

"It doesn't have to be what it looks like," she said, still wanting to be wrong. "What if he's involved in some op you and I don't know about? An SD-6 op, I mean."

"It's possible," Noah conceded. His eyes hardened. "But it's not likely."

"I just don't want to get him in trouble if he's not doing anything wrong. Wilson's like . . ." Squeezing her eyes shut against rising tears, Sydney drew in a shuddering breath. "He's important to me."

"I understand. But you were right to call me," Noah assured her, tucking the drive into his coat. "This has to be reported."

"Right now? Maybe the two of us could deal with this ourselves—just until we're certain. Wilson doesn't know I saw him tonight. We could shadow him. Set up surveillance and stakeouts and—"

"Not this time." Noah shook his head sadly. "I'm sorry, Sydney, but this has to go higher. You know it does."

Hot tears escaped her eyes at last. "I don't even know who to report it to."

Noah put his arms around her again and rested his cheek on her head. "You've already reported it—to me. I'll take it from here."

"Who are you going to tell?"

"Someone who'll know what to do. I'll take this program back to headquarters, make my report, and then . . ."

"What?" she asked desperately.

"We'll have to wait and see. For your sake, I hope this is some sort of mix-up, but . . ." He shrugged against her body. "Whatever happens will be over soon."

"I just . . . Will Wilson go to prison?"

"We'll have to see," he repeated, smoothing her hair away from her face. "But now I have to go." He turned her loose and stepped away, his expression full of purpose.

"I'll let you know what happens," he added. "And if SD-6 needs your help, I'll call you. But for now it's out of your hands. Try not to worry about it."

Sydney nodded mutely and watched him walk off into the darkness, Wilson's fate in his coat pocket.

Noah was right: It *was* out of her hands. For better or worse, she'd set something in motion that she couldn't stop. If Wilson was innocent, he was going to know she'd betrayed him. And if he was guilty . . .

Sydney covered her face, afraid to finish the thought. "What have I done?" she moaned.

To: tchristian@cia.gov

From: rlw@free-mailboxes.com

Subject: Urgent

Did something go wrong with the drop? Why haven't you returned my messages? Respond ASAP.

14

I CAN'T DO THIS, Sydney thought, arriving on the main floor of SD-6 the next afternoon. *I won't.*

But she hadn't been given a choice. Noah had made his report and word had come back from on high: There was no secret SD-6 operation. Wilson was a traitor.

Noah's instructions to her on the phone could not have been more clear. The brass at SD-6 wanted Wilson taken into custody, but not inside headquarters. If he decided to shoot it out, too many people could get hurt. Snatching him at his home had been ruled against as too public and likely to fail. Instead, they would have an armed security team apprehend him inside a deserted downtown building.

It was Sydney's job to lure him there.

"Why me?" she'd protested when Noah told her the news. "Why can't someone else do it?"

"Because Wilson trusts you," he'd replied.

"That's exactly why I don't want to be involved!"

But in the end he'd convinced her. Wilson was going to be picked up anyway; she owed it to her colleagues to make sure no one got hurt in the process.

Not even Wilson.

Not that he's likely to appreciate it, she thought, striding down the hall to his office. *I'm not expecting gratitude.*

She didn't know what to expect.

"Sydney!" Wilson exclaimed when she appeared in his doorway. "I told you to take the day off today."

"Something's come up," she said. At least she didn't have to fake the worry in her voice. "I think someone's spying on me."

"What?" Wilson's brows drew together in a way she might once have confused with concern. "Who?"

"I don't know. But Owen Vincent's still out there, right? And presumably he has friends."

"We can't arrest him now," Wilson said. "Without the missile software, we've got nothing."

"Yeah. It's a shame how that turned out." She forced herself to meet his eyes. "Still, Kristin Jarvis disappeared kind of suddenly. Maybe he put two and two together."

"Do you really believe he has you under surveillance? Tell me exactly what you saw."

I saw you drop that hard drive into a trash can! she wanted to scream.

She took a deep breath instead.

"This guy's started following me around campus," she said. "I got suspicious and tracked him to a building a few miles from here, but the place is deserted. He walked in and disappeared."

"People don't just disappear, Sydney."

"They do if they're spies."

Wilson smiled. "You have a point. But there must be an outlet you didn't find. A secret exit somewhere."

"I know. Can you come help me look for it?"

She had done it. The question hung between them. Sydney held her breath, half hoping he'd say no.

Wilson grimaced. "Now?"

"Could you? Maybe it's nothing, but if this guy

knows who I am, and he knows where I live . . . I won't sleep until I find out what's going on."

"I can't leave the office now, Sydney. Let's call in Agent Hicks to help you."

"It's almost five o'clock," she said, having anticipated this objection. "And I'd rather have you."

"Really?" Wilson raised a skeptical brow. "I thought you and Noah had hit it off."

"What are you talking about?" she said, embarrassed. "He never even talks to me!"

"Hence my suspicion," he said with a wry smile.

"Noah's all right," Sydney admitted, making Wilson's smile even broader. "But he's hotheaded. He rushes into things, like that SST disaster. I'd feel safer if you came with me."

Wilson looked worried again. "You honestly think you're in danger?"

"Maybe. I don't know. Will you come?"

This time he didn't hesitate.

"Of course," he said, grabbing his jacket.

* * *

In her car on the way to the rendezvous point, Sydney was in agony. If Wilson had refused to come with her, the burden of his capture would have shifted to someone else. But there he was, riding cluelessly in her passenger seat, full of apparent concern about whether someone was trying to hurt her.

Which only makes this harder.

SD-6 brass had been right about Wilson; he cared about her. If he didn't, would he be letting her drag him off on such a wild-goose chase? He trusted her.

And she was about to betray him.

No! she thought, sneaking a sideways glance at her recruiter. *He's the one who betrayed us!*

But nothing she told herself could make what she was doing feel right. SD-6 had guessed how much Wilson cared about her; they didn't seem to realize how much she cared about Wilson. He had believed in her when no one else had. He'd recruited a shy, lonely freshman and turned her into something more than she'd ever dreamed she could be. He had trained her, nurtured her, kicked her butt when she needed it. . . .

He wasn't her father—he was closer than that.

I love him, she thought, nearly choking on her guilt.

"So, how's school?" Wilson asked obliviously. "Are you caught up in your classes yet?"

"Pretty much. I should be by the end of the week, anyway." Something told her she was about to have a lot of time on her hands.

"It's amazing the way you balance your school schedule with everything you do for SD-6," he said. "Everyone at the agency's in awe. I should have told you that before."

"It's not that hard," Sydney lied, mortified. Now he wanted to *praise* her?

"When I was a freshman, I couldn't even balance my classes with my drinking binges. You're so much more mature than that."

"Well . . . you know . . . ," she said uncomfortably. "Girls mature faster than boys."

Wilson laughed. "Yes. So girls keep telling us."

Sydney could see her target office building up ahead, and the long, empty stretch of curb in front of it. Business hours had ended for the day, which explained why most of the surrounding buildings looked vacant too. She guided her car toward a spot at the curb, wishing the whole experience were over.

She hit the brakes harder than she'd intended, rocking them both in their seats. The Mustang stopped two feet from the curb.

Wilson raised an eyebrow. "Remind me to always wear my seat belt with you."

He opened his car door and stepped into the dry gutter. Sydney gripped the wheel a moment longer, then abruptly jumped out too. A warm wind blew down the street, pushing scraps of paper before it. She breathed in the scents of summer and smog, the entire situation unreal.

Wilson was already waiting for her by the entrance.

"It's unlocked," she said, reaching past him for the doorknob. "At least it was before."

The door swung open, revealing a small, dark lobby with grimy walls and soiled carpeting. There was no furniture, only a few coils of abandoned computer cable lying on the floor.

"This doesn't look too promising," he observed. "What's in back?"

Don't go in back! Sydney had to fight the impulse to shout it out loud. *Turn around, Wilson. Turn around and run!*

"Storage racks and a loading dock," she said.

"Better. Let's look there."

She watched him walk through the lobby, everything seeming to happen in slow motion. Her heart pounded, her lips moved, but she was frozen in place. He reached for the back door. His hand closed over the knob.

"Wilson?" she blurted out.

He paused, turning to look at her. "Yes, Sydney?"

The door flew open, pulled hard from the other side. Wilson staggered back with it, and before he could catch his balance, four black-clad men were on him, pinning his arms and legs and stripping his sidearm from under his jacket.

"Run, Sydney!" he cried, struggling frantically. "Get out!"

But she just stood there. Frozen.

Wilson tried to fight, but he couldn't get any leverage. One of the masked agents wrestled cuffs onto his wrists, clamping them down savagely. Another punched Wilson in the stomach, and he crumpled to his knees. The security squad was terrifying, a study in black body armor, full ski masks, and anonymous intimidation. If Sydney hadn't known they were the good guys, she'd have thought they were dragging Wilson off to his execution.

Wilson looked up at her, his face twisted with pain. "Run, Sydney," he pleaded again.

He didn't know she couldn't run, couldn't move, could barely even breathe. She seemed to be watching from outside her body as Wilson was dragged backward into the warehouse area.

And finally the light clicked on in his eyes.

"You brought me here. . . . You told them I . . .

No, Sydney! It's not what you think! None of this is what you think!"

She tried to speak, couldn't find any words.

"I'm not a traitor, I swear!" Wilson insisted desperately, struggling against his captors. "You have to believe me, Sydney. I—"

One of the agents punched him in the jaw, cutting off his protestations.

Sydney watched with tears rolling down her face as Wilson was forced into the back of a waiting van and two guards jumped in behind him. A third man slammed the van doors shut, cutting off the sounds of the skirmish inside, while the fourth got into the driver's seat and revved up the engine. A moment later, they were gone, leaving the loading dock door gaping open like a giant screaming mouth.

Sydney collapsed to the lobby floor, her legs folding beneath her. The tears in her eyes blurred the empty place where Wilson had just been, but they were already drying, replaced by a strange sense of calm.

Her heart had almost betrayed her, her body had failed her completely, but her brain was now certain she'd done the right thing.

Whatever feelings she might have had for Wilson, seeing his arrest had set her straight. To hear him lie that way, right to her face, all the while begging with those pleading eyes . . . it was enough to make her sick.

I did the right thing, she thought. *Whatever SD-6 does to Wilson now, it won't be on my conscience. He was a traitor, and I turned him in.*

She took a deep breath and let it out slowly.

I protected my country.

15

SYDNEY STUMBLED INTO HER dorm room and
fell facedown on her bed, collapsing into sobs. She
couldn't hold back the tears anymore—she didn't
even want to. They overtook her in waves, racking
her whole body.

"Sydney!" Francie cried, jumping up from her
desk. "What happened?"

She opened her mouth to speak, but there was
nothing she could say. More sobs rose up instead,
nearly choking her.

The bed dipped as Francie sat beside her, tentatively touching her shoulder. "Syd? Where have you been? Work?"

She had been downtown, betraying her handler and the one man she knew cared about her . . . but she couldn't tell that to Francie. She could barely admit it to herself. Wilson had turned against SD-6, but he'd never been *her* enemy. The momentary peace she'd found in the abandoned building had completely deserted her now, replaced by the heartbreaking knowledge that she'd never see Wilson again.

Francie gasped at a sudden thought. "They didn't . . . did they fire you?"

Still facedown, Sydney shook her head.

"Then what?" Francie demanded. "You're starting to scare me, Syd. Did somebody hurt you?"

Sydney shook her head again. "No," she finally forced out. "Nothing like that. I'm sorry."

Francie's hand found Sydney's back, rubbing in small, comforting circles. "Just tell me what's going on."

"Nothing." Another hiccupping sob. "Stress."

"You poor thing. If anyone ever earned a little nervous breakdown, it's you." Francie's hand stopped rubbing. "It is a *little* breakdown, right? I mean, I don't need to call Health Services?"

"No, don't," Sydney said, still crying but not as hard.

"If you think about it, we should have seen this coming. Between finals and all the extra hours you've been working for the bank, and now having your father in town, it's no surprise you're having a meltdown."

"Yeah." Sydney grabbed a tissue off the nightstand. "It's been hard."

"You know what you need?" Francie said. "A night off."

"You're probably right." She was too upset to study anyway. "Do you want to hang out? Maybe watch *Star Wars*?"

"Again?" Francie smiled. "I think we can do better than that. Why don't I call Burke and—"

"No!" Sydney said, sitting up. "Don't call Burke."

"Why not? You said he was complaining about never seeing you, and it will cheer you up, too."

"I can't deal with Burke right now."

"Is there something wrong between you two?" Francie asked, confused. "Something you haven't told me?"

There were so many things Sydney hadn't told her . . . and so many lies she had. She felt like she was drowning in her secret life.

"I'm going to break things off with Burke

tomorrow." The words seemed to come out of nowhere, shocking her as much as Francie.

Francie stood up and stared with disbelief. "What? When did you decide that?"

"Just now," Sydney said slowly, realizing she meant it. "I should have done it a while ago, but I really like Burke and I thought if I gave us more time . . . The problem is Burke doesn't know me."

"Because you're never around!" Francie said. "That's what he's been trying to tell—"

"I'm in love with somebody else."

"What?" Francie reached behind her, groping her way to a seat on her own bed. "With *who*?"

"His name is Noah."

"Noah *who*?"

"Noah Hicks."

"I can't believe this." Francie peered at Sydney as if she might be imagining things. "Burke really likes you. And now you're going to dump him for some guy you've barely met?"

"Actually? I met Noah before Burke."

"But you've been seeing Burke for weeks! I've never even heard of this Noah!" Francie's voice was starting to sound more annoyed than amazed.

"I know. I would have mentioned him before, but—"

"Let me guess," Francie interrupted bitterly. "You've been too busy."

"I didn't want to say anything because I don't know where things are going with Noah. Or if they're going anywhere."

"I thought we were best friends."

"We are." Sydney heaved a tired sigh. "It's just . . . complicated."

"And you love this guy?" Francie demanded.

Sydney hesitated a second, waiting for the doubt to hit, but all she felt was relief. "I do."

"You're just full of surprises tonight," Francie said, every trace of her earlier sympathy gone.

"You're mad at me now."

"Not mad. I'm just hurt that you don't trust me."

"That's not true! I trust you completely."

"Whatever." Francie raised an ominous brow. "Burke's the one who's going to kill you."

* * *

In five minutes this will all be over, Sydney reassured herself, clutching her history textbook tighter. *I'm doing the right thing.*

But that didn't keep her stomach from aching as the students in Professor Baldridge's American history lecture surged to their feet, marking the end of the morning class. She had slipped in late and taken a seat in back to avoid dealing with Burke, but she couldn't postpone their encounter any longer—he was headed directly for her.

"Hey!" he said, stopping just inches away. His shaggy red hair was endearingly messy, and a growth of stubble accentuated his square chin. "I saved you a seat in front. What's the deal sitting way back here?"

"I just . . . I was late and . . . Can we talk about this outside?"

"Talk about what?" he asked, not budging.

The probing way his eyes held hers made her feel kind of dizzy. "I can't breathe in here," she said. "Please. Let's go outside." She turned and led the way out of the lecture hall, half hoping he wouldn't follow.

Ending things with him had seemed like the right thing to do the night before. But if he walked the other way now, she wouldn't have to give the little speech she'd prepared, wouldn't have to see his face when he heard the news, wouldn't have to feel worse than she already did. . . .

When she turned around on the pavement outside the building, though, Burke was right behind her. She walked over a patch of grass and stopped beneath a jacaranda tree, looking for more privacy.

"What's this about? You're acting weird." He pushed his hands deep into the pockets of his jeans, the gesture betraying his growing unease. "Is something wrong?"

She tried to smile, but it hurt too much.

"You know I really like you, right?" she got out finally. "But lately I've felt like I'm letting you down. Like we're not really clicking."

"How can you say that?" he asked, wounded. "I'm crazy about you."

"But—but—" she stammered. "You're always complaining I'm not around enough. And I can't be, Burke—not the way you want me to. The truth is, I don't know what I'm doing this summer. I don't even know what I'm doing later on today."

"This is about your job, isn't it?" His eyes had clouded with pain, but his voice was still steady. "I haven't been understanding enough about—"

"No," she cut in quickly. "I mean, yes. My job's a big part of it. But you've been plenty understanding. That's not it."

"Then what?" He reached forward and squeezed her hands. "Tell me what the problem is and I'll fix it."

He looked so sincere, so completely genuine,

that Sydney began to cry. Big silent tears welled up and spilled over her lashes.

He deserved so much better than this.

"I just . . . don't think we're right for each other. You're such a great guy. I hope we'll still be friends. But you'll be better off with a different girl—a girl who can be there one hundred percent."

"Oh, no," he said, a defiant spark catching in his hazel eyes. "You're not going to break up with me for my own good. I can take care of myself, all right?"

"I know you can." She was so ashamed she could barely look at him. When she did, fresh tears blurred her vision, dripping off her chin. "I just can't do this anymore."

"But I still don't understand. I mean, if I didn't do anything wrong . . ." He let go of her hands abruptly, taking a big step backward.

"Is there someone else?" he asked flatly.

She hadn't wanted to tell him that. Even if Noah didn't exist, she and Burke would never be able to have an honest relationship. She'd lied to him so much already. . . .

He deserved the truth.

"Yes," she whispered, dropping her gaze to the grass. "I'm sorry."

"How long?" he asked in a strangled voice.

"A few . . . weeks."

"You liar!" he exclaimed, the unleashed anger in his tone making Sydney wince. "All those excuses about how you had to work and the whole time you were running around with someone else!"

"No, I *was* working."

"I'm so stupid! Sitting around waiting for you, believing everything you said."

"Burke, it wasn't—"

"What else have you lied about, Sydney? That trip to Hawaii you supposedly went on with Francie? The late-night filing? Do you even have a job?"

Every word was like a slap in the face.

"Of course I have a job!"

"How am I supposed to know? If you'll lie about one thing . . ."

"I was working," she insisted. "And I never said there wasn't someone else." It was a pathetic argument; she knew that the second it came out of her mouth.

"Oh, good. That makes it okay, then," he said sarcastically.

"Of course it doesn't. That was a dumb thing to—"

"You know what? I think you were right after all. We're not clicking. You're not even the girl I thought you were. Turns out all this time I was falling for a completely different person. And the joke's on me, because so were you."

"Please, Burke. I care about you so much," she began, but he cut her off.

"Don't waste your time," he said. "I won't believe you anyway."

She recoiled as if he had hit her. For a moment, his expression twisted with pain and she glimpsed the Burke she had known before—sweet, sensitive, open. Then he turned on his heel and walked away.

Sydney watched him go, feeling worse than she'd ever imagined.

She had hurt him. She had lost his friendship forever.

And there wasn't one thing he'd accused her of that wasn't completely true.

* * *

I don't care anymore, Sydney thought miserably, letting herself into her empty dorm room. *I don't even care if I fail every single final.*

She threw herself down on her bed, unable to face the rest of her classes. In less than twenty-four hours she had completely destroyed her relationships with both Wilson and Burke, and she was starting to think it was all her fault. If only she'd handled things differently, maybe she could have salvaged Wilson somehow. There was no question she'd treated Burke horribly, and the knowledge filled her with self-loathing. She just needed to be alone, to have some space to sort things out. . . .

And then the telephone rang.

I'm not picking that up, she thought.

There was no one she wanted to talk to. Besides, the call was probably for Francie.

The answering machine clicked on: "Hey! This is Francie and Sydney. You know what to do!"

A loud beep followed, then a voice.

"Sydney? This is your father."

She groaned, knowing she ought to pick up the line but too depressed to talk.

"Listen, something's come up at work. I have to leave town kind of suddenly."

She rolled over and started to reach for the phone. If he was leaving, she *had* to talk to him now; otherwise she might miss their last chance to get together.

"Actually, I'm calling from a pay phone at the airport. Sorry I didn't get to say good-bye in person, but this is important."

Sydney froze with her hand in the air. Of *course* it was important—his stupid job was always more important than she was.

"Anyway, I hope all goes well with your finals,

and I'll try to call in a week or two. You, um . . . You take care."

The dial tone sounded. She didn't even have a number to call him back.

Why would I want to? she wondered, pulling a pillow over her head. She'd thought her fight with Burke had left her out of tears, but now she discovered that she'd been wrong. They wet her cheeks and pillow, making her even more wretched than before.

Just stop it. You knew he'd do this—or something like it. He always does.

But it still hurt. And more than she'd expected.

She'd honestly believed he was trying this time. Despite their arguing, she'd thought they were making some progress. Now she felt like a fool.

She'd let him in, and he'd let her down. Again. Just one more vacancy in her life—first Wilson, then Burke, now him . . .

How did he always manage to leave her right when she needed him most?

No more, she vowed, crying into her pillow. *Never again—that's it.*

The next time my father is in L.A., I'm *going to Brazil!*

16

"JUST TELL ME WHO sent this," Sydney whispered nervously, showing Noah her pager. HQ CR ASAP was displayed on its tiny screen.

"It could have been anyone," he replied.

She had been thrilled to find him at a desk when she walked past the bull pen at SD-6, but beyond the news that *CR* stood for conference room, Noah hadn't been able to shed any light on her situation. He just happened to be there that afternoon, working a normal shift.

"It *couldn't* be anyone," she argued, "because

the only people who have this number are you and Wilson. You don't think *Wilson*—?"

"Definitely not," he assured her quickly. "There are a few other people."

"Like who?"

She had expected to get a summons from SD-6 eventually, but she'd also expected it to come from Noah. So ever since her beeper had gone off an hour before, rousing her from a tear-induced nap, she'd been making herself crazy wondering what it meant.

"There are . . . people," Noah said vaguely. "I can't give you names."

"Why not?"

He glanced out over the floor, his message clear. Headquarters was full of agents that Wednesday; it was impossible to know who might be listening.

Sydney lowered her voice even further. "Will you be here? After I find out what's going on, I mean."

"I'll wait for you," he whispered back, barely any sound to the words. "I was going to call you tonight anyway. I thought you might want to talk about"—he glanced around again—"things."

She gave him a grateful smile, reassured. She'd made so many mistakes, but somehow Noah was still in her life. That, at least, she'd gotten right.

Walking to the conference room, though,

Sydney felt her moment of peace slipping away. She had no idea who had paged her, or why, and it wasn't a good feeling. She took a seat in one of the room's black leather chairs, not put more at ease by the fact that the lights were off and all the monitors were dark.

Are they going to fire me? she wondered, fidgeting. Now that Wilson was gone, she didn't have a handler. Maybe no one else had time for a trainee. Or perhaps Wilson's fall had tainted them both. If there was a procedure for dealing with this situation, she had no clue what it was.

Maybe leaving SD-6 wouldn't be such a bad thing.

The thought surprised her, but only for a moment. She still wanted to help make the world a better place, but since she'd joined the CIA, everything else in her life had suffered. Her relationships, her social life, her schoolwork . . . even her family life, such as it was.

If they show me the door, I won't beg to stay, she decided. *I've made enough money to last for a while—especially with Dad so determined to pay my expenses. I could go to London after all.*

SD-6 wouldn't be the same without Wilson anyway. It was painful even to sit in the same room where she'd met him for so many briefings. She could almost see him at the head of the table, getting ready to send her off on some exciting new mission. Like her first one, to Paris, when he'd popped open that suitcase filled with designer clothes . . . He'd seemed too good to be true then.

Now she'd never see him again.

I wonder what they're doing with him? But almost as quickly, her mind blocked the question. She kept telling herself it wasn't her fault, but she couldn't think of Wilson in prison, maybe even in shackles, without feeling partly to blame. Whatever he was going through, she didn't want to know.

The lights switched on overhead, making Sydney start in her seat. She turned her head in time to see a fatherly man walk into the room, a huge, warm smile on his clean-shaven face. It was the man she had met when first recruited into SD-6, the man Wilson had introduced her to.

Arvin Sloane.

Something about his presence pulled her up out of her chair. He had such energy . . . and it was all focused on her.

"Sydney!" he said, extending his hand. "We meet again. I've heard such fantastic things about your work."

She smiled uncertainly and put her hand in his. His skin felt warm and dry as he pumped her arm up and down, full of enthusiasm.

"I hope they were true," she said.

"All true," he assured her jovially. "I check those reports personally."

His face took on a more somber expression. "Shall we sit?" he asked, gesturing to a couple of chairs and waiting for her to take one.

"Before we go any further," he said, "I want you to know I realize you've been through hell the past few days. Reg Wilson's betrayal was a terrible shock to us all. But, thanks to you, that threat has been dealt with and SD-6 has recovered some crucial intelligence. I'll be taking over as your new handler."

"You, uh . . . you still want me to work here, then?"

"Of course! More than ever!" He seemed genuinely shocked she could have thought anything else. "This is a lifetime organization, Sydney. We're like a family."

"But Wilson . . ."

"Yes, I know. Terrible," Sloane said, shaking his head. "Sometimes people do leave us. But we never, ever turn our backs on our own."

His dark eyes held hers a moment, letting her

see the deep sadness Wilson's defection had caused him.

"No," she murmured, struck by his intensity. "We wouldn't do that."

"We're a good organization, Sydney. A *strong* organization. Stick with me, and I'll take you places. We'll make a killer team."

"I will," she said, abandoning her thoughts of leaving SD-6. "I mean, thank you, Mr. Sloane. I'd like that."

"Call me Arvin," he said.

"Okay . . . Arvin."

He beamed as if they'd accomplished something important, and all the worry inside Sydney lay down, finally at rest. She returned his happy smile, overcome with relief.

Arvin Sloane seemed strong, capable, warm. He not only understood how she felt about losing Wilson, he felt the same way. And, best of all, he believed in her. He wanted to be a family, a team. He wanted to take her places.

Maybe she'd finally found the man who could fill the hole in her life.

Things in this circus never go as planned. I did my best in Los Angeles, but Sydney's stuck deep into SD-6. She honestly believes she's part of the **real** CIA.

I wish to God she were.

But I can't tell her the truth. The only thing more deadly than working for Arvin Sloane is working against him.

Reginald Wilson nearly found that out the hard way.

I wish I had a picture of his face at the extraction, after I released the rest of the SD-6 team and drove him into the desert. Well, not exactly then, but a couple of hours later, when I let him out of the cuffs and he finally realized that I'm with the CIA too. Up until that moment, he'd been sure I was going to kill him.

Arvin, of course, believes that I did.

I'll admit it—part of me wanted to. Punching him in the mouth certainly felt good. If only I could have shut him up back in September, before he dragged Sydney into this mess . . .

But Sloane would have recruited my daughter with or without his help. Now all I can do is wait for my chance to bail us both out. Another year, maybe. Two, at the most . . .

Reg was right about one thing: My daughter's an exceptional girl.

Wilson's a seasoned agent, and my trainee daughter had him. **Totally** had him. He never saw it coming. Not only that, but I watched her pick up a CIA drop and just generally screw up a whole lot of plans on both sides of the law.

So while I'd be happier if she'd never heard of SD-6, at least now I know she can hold her own. She's smart, she's well trained, and, best of all, she's suspicious. I'm pretty sure she pegged me watching her that day in the park—not that she guessed that homeless man was me. She seems incapable of seeing me as anything other than a workaholic salesman.

I've never let her down in that role, at least.

But someday soon she'll know the truth. Her mother's death, my unavoidable absences, and how hard I've tried to set everything right, to give her a chance at a normal life . . .

I may not be much of a father figure, but I've always been her **father**.

DANGER AROUND
EVERY CURVE.

ALIAS™
THE GAME
ALIASTHEGAME.COM

Touchstone Television

ACClaim®
www.acclaim.com

PlayStation®2

XBOX

BUENA
VISTA
INTERACTIVE